– *ACKNOWLEDGMENTS* –

A listing of prior periodical publication of poems can be found in the back of this book, and of course, thanks are due to the editors.

Lines from "My Mother's Pears," are from Stanley Kunitz, *Passing Through: The Later Poems New and Selected*, W.W. Norton & Co, 1995, p. 142.

Sylvia Plath's poem about a goose is "Rhyme," from *The Collected Poems of Sylvia Plath*, Harper & Row, 1981, p. 50.

Lines from Elizabeth Bishop are from "The Man-Moth," and "Questions of Travel," *The Complete Poems 1927-1979*, Farrar, Straus, Giroux, 1988, pp. 14 and 93.

The epigraph is from Henry Miller, *Black Spring*, Grove Press, 1963, p. 76.

Poems copyright © 2000 by Ruth Moon Kempher
Illustrations © copyright 2000 by Wayne Hogan

ISBN # 1-888832-13-4

KINGS ESTATE PRESS
870 Kings Estate Road
St. Augustine, FL 32086-5033

kep@aug.com

Watermark Angels

poetry by
Ruth Moon Kempher

illustrations by
Wayne Hogan

Kings Estate Press, 2000
St. Augustine, Florida

Watermark Angels

WATERMARK ANGELS

The angel is there to lead you to Heaven, where it is all plus and no minus. The angel is there like a watermark, a guarantee of your faultless vision. ... The angel is there to drop sprigs of parsley in your omelette, to put a shamrock in your buttonhole.

Henry Miller, *Black Spring*

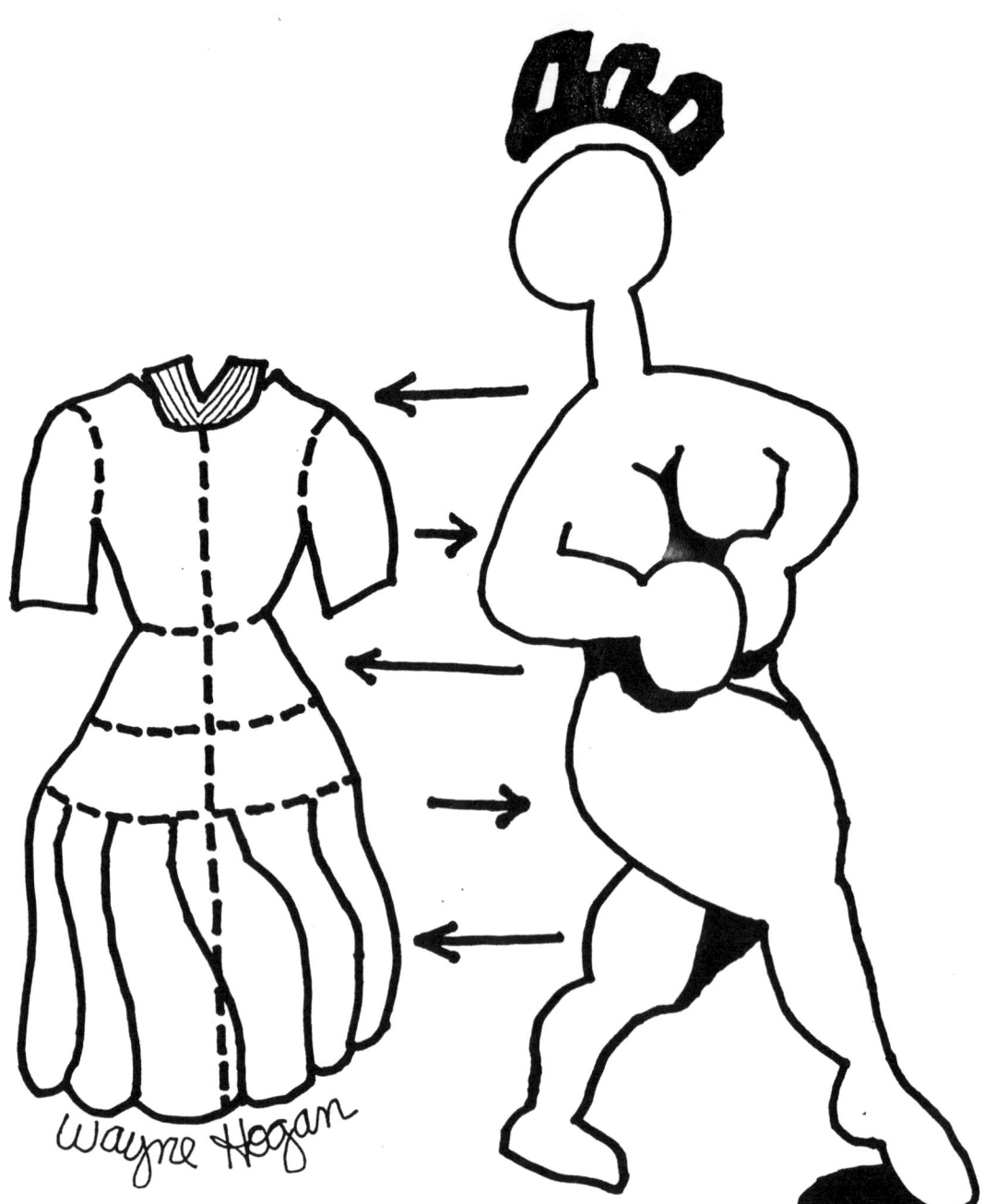

– TABLE OF CONTENTS –

PART ONE: OF THE NURSERY

  1. Gambit
  2. Terns
  3. Apple Lyric
  4. 'More Apples! ...'
  5. Eve's Tart Answer
  6.   / Her Coda: A Liturgy
  7. White Herons, from Sunday, Monday
 11. Quince, on Susanna's List
 12. The Woodcutter's Secrets Revealed
 13. The Cock Robin Episode ...
 17. The Three Little Pigs and Their Diets
 19. An Eternal Triangle: Hansel and Gretel ...
 22. The Vine Fable
 23. You're Quite Sure Then, That You Have Grown Up?
 24. Cinderella Said To Her Ugly Stepsister
 25. The Chased: A Revision
 28. Uncle Ike, Mover and Shaper
 29. Two Mother Poems—Gertrude's Poem
 30.   / Found Poem: My Mother, the Typist
 31. Flying to Gatwick, She Drifts ...

PART TWO: OF THE CLASSROOM, AND THE HOUSE

 33. Leda, in the Classroom
 34. On the Way
 35. She Steals a Metaphor ...
 37. Watching a Movie and Writing a Poem
 39. Slides: Room 6C, Dr. Dobrovsky's Summer Vacation ...
 41. Looking Up "Ecpyrosis"
 42. Looking for Kierkegaard / In a Strange Novel
 43. Thursday's Poem
 45. The Old Dog
 46. Moment, Apocalyptic ...
 47. From the Tub, She Teaches ...
 48. What Lola—A Dog Brought Up on Wallace Stevens ...

49. The Inventory Queen
51. Once, When I Was Esther Williams
52. Presuming on Emily's #341
53. Beginning Her Clearly Mad, Unfinished Journal ...
57. Two Good Bitch Poems
58. Listening to Your Song, Studying

PART THREE: OF TRAVELS, FIELD TRIPS TAKEN OR DREAMED

59. Looking for D.H. Lawrence, in Taormina
60. She Interviews D.H. Lawrence / Not Either in Heaven ...
61. Kiosk / Gazebo
64. Unofficial Log: *S.S. Orizaba* ...
65. Though Pagan at Heart, She Celebrates ...
66. In Real Life, as in the Theatre ...
67. Reading about Boswell's Clap ...
69. Wayside Flowers, Well
71. In Renoir's Diningroom
73. Her Matisse Notes
74. Certain Picassos Bring Back Great Fear ...
75. The Doormat Variations
83. Key West / Stevens Paper: First Notes
85. Post Card Jotting:
86. The Perpetual Moth
87. Questioning Travel
89. Mile-Marker #1, U S 1, Key West
92. In Robert Frost's Key West Garden
96. Mr. Dillon, Etc.
98. Pole Beans and Fences
100. Night Fevers, and Some Flowers
103. The Hawk
105. Pavlova's Dogs
106. Prufrock, on the Stairs
107. Having in Mind Only Communication ...

PART ONE:
OF THE NURSERY

GAMBIT

Liebling, said Bluebeard, Trust me
but stay the hell out of my closet

and whoever it was who gave Pandora
the box full of beautiful itchings

Trust me, look at the etchings, but
don't turn that key. Well, honestly

anytime anyone's said to me, Don't
I've thought I will before I won't.

TERNS

Sky begins
like an alphabet
beginning with b—
blue nursery walls
and always birds

                whirling—
                a world in words
                sounding crisp
                flitter of feathers
                sunlit robins
                or sparrows

no terns or herons
but take a trip
in the wooden swan's
awkward passage
on blue linoleum
a sea voyage

                yellow tiny birds
                in the chinaberry bush
                ticked at the window
                telling vowels
                O yes, an ash weight
                like innocence
                gone.

APPLE LYRIC

Cut into
the apple releases

acid clean, that scent
motif of warning—

windfall visions, thin twigs
poking into a pale sky

and the cricket beneath
who splashes "Repent!"

on the rubble of mountains—
pips, kernels, an ancient comfort—

at apple's center floats a star.

"MORE APPLES! ALWAYS APPLES!" CRIES THE CRITIC

as he tells me, sighing, there are more allusions to apples
in manuscripts and books, than this world dreams of—
taking inventory, he says there are enough, but

his eye reflects, dapple green and goat-grained, a madness
delighted by lists: summations of covet and lust, those
                wind-fall gifts of grandparents ...

somewhere he's missed the point. Buried by ledgers, whose
leather-bound pages are recovered with scratch seascapes
wormed cross-stitch by silverfish, he insists

"More apples than anyone could wish, and as for cider—"
waves his hands as if he'd brush away visions, fat
                apples plumping into grass ...

vine-veined hands, whose mindless task
is cribbing presents from the past.

EVE'S TART ANSWER

"Apples, apples,"
cries Eve. "It's always
something about apples they taunt me with—
                  some acid grief
as if even these
peeled, sliced and parboiled by machine
(untouched by human hands)
        descended from that first. I'm even sick
of apple poems, puns on pomes—

comfort me with cinnamon, for I am sick
                  or cloves
for love's sake, black rosettes fine ground, O
smell, divine tang that smoothes the air
a gift—O, globe, a bitter pomander
to gentle the landlord ...

    Remember the old orchard?
the brook that tumbled, snaked
through the pomegranate groves ...
how we felt harried sometimes, even cursed.
There, the worst crimes (already) were those
of dispossession—how the birds
nudged against each other, bees
fumbled in the marigolds

and those bridal flowers, bright against the sky
became fruit, so unexpected.

                      Now it's an old joke
the Adam's apple protrudent, obscene
ideas of crabbed apples, omens
of old age, wrinkles ...
blame it all on apples ...
troubled, we were, even in clothes.

It was only, you know, after apples came
the new gifts—tears' release
and better, laughter."

HER CODA: A LITURGY

Think, how the world is
an apple, hung
in a dark closet—

think, how it rots
hanging, ' til nowhere's
left

to shove it. Think
how the worm
loves it.

WHITE HERONS, FROM SUNDAY, SEEN MONDAY

1.

three surfers hunch up, out where the water raises
a ridge that curls and crumples
white surf
and porpoise feeding
banging the water with their chins

        Eve, O Eve in forgotten Eden
        dabbled in leaf-lined water
        and this tang of salt—
        found brine

a mullet fisher's net blooms explosive in middle distance
surprises space and light
blue sky
its containment shimmering
with mute clangor, muffled cries

        Eve, in her seashell necklace
        fingered the fragile rib racks
        fish left behind—
        saw signs

I and the old dog wander, here in places
sand scours, at proper tides
green pools

find in sea-scum a heron
fishing on one leg, one claw tucked up high

> Eve, and those fish found flying
> touched by the hand of Adam
> and a healthy hunger
> tasted Time.

2.

Sunday, lavender crabs danced tip-claw
blue-veined, on a marsh-mired shingle
green vines
tangled overhead, reflected
with reflections of heron, knuckle to knuckle

> I, wondering where heron days
> and all clear water vanish
> in half-earnest anger
> taste brine

how that heron stalked his own image, saw
himself recurring in ever deeper
blue ripples
dappled water, chased after—
like Narcissus—that taunting shadow

> I, with the old dog haunched beside
> muscle-tight with tension
> with another noon coming up
> see signs

O, bewitched by wonders, if Sunday's heron drowning there
resurfaced here, a mirror image
white feathers
feigning father, or brother
more solid in murk of surf-suds, up for air

    I, in sand that gnaws my feet
    mull over heron on heron, seen
    in water-mirrored sky
    find Time.

QUINCE, ON SUSANNA'S LIST

They dined on mince, and slices of quince.
    Edward Lear, "The Owl and the Pussycat"

"And," Susanna laughs, "There will be leftovers
forever." She dances, not to music, but
Moon's light, her elders
fled in disarray.
    Bottom notes, relentless
from Phoenix City: "One of the stranger places
for a banjo is one's knee."

    Susanna remembers
how like a loon, or owl-eyed in his innocence
poor Quince had strayed. The wrong spoon
for instance, taken from the *hors d'oeuvres* tray ...
"Runcible," she murmurs. Remembers crackers
with small jellies, and paté. "That trio—
Bottom, Moon and Quince of better days—

The runcible spoon is NOT for rarebit. Blobs
slipped from its three broad tines, remain
like watermarks coiled, ring-a-leavy
where he set his drink down." Not to say
caviar, on the keys.

    "Still," she sways. "Beauty
IS 'momentary in the mind. ...'" And purrs:
"I shall have him here again, to play."

THE WOODCUTTER'S SECRETS REVEALED

Finger crooked, dark dense eyes, like forest undergrowth—
"Confidentially," he whispers, "I'm poor. I'm nervous
and certifiably over-sensitive concerning my deficiencies;
not to mention trembling in my boots. That is,"

he giggles. "I'm not sure which witch was or is the worse.
Believe me, I verge on agoraphobia. It's all that gingerbread,"
cocking an effete eyebrow. "The one who fancied herself
a baker was gross. A dreadful house; and the heat of her oven.

To top it off, one unzipped the belly of yon wolf, and out
pops Red Riding Hood's Granny. A shock. My nerves.
You've no idea what THAT did to my blood pressure.
My hernia hurts. Indeed, I swooned. What do I wake up to?

Chapter and verse. She's another witch—I stand accused.
An ogre. I've violated the rights of her wolf! O, she tells me
he had a horrible, deprived childhood. HE was abused!
I should have left her inside him, stewing."

He sighs. "After all this time, I'm still unkiltered, out of sorts.
I may say in truth, I'm cursed. Kin am I, well in accord with
those child-encumbered Snow Whites in the Laundromat
whose eyes say, Ever After should come first."

THE COCK ROBIN EPISODE: AN INCOMPLETE
CLOSET / INTERIOR DRAMA, ON SEVERAL STAGES

Where I left off, let me begin again.
    Geoffrey Chaucer, *The Canterbury Tales*

LADY SOLO [sighing]: When last on stage, ah Love, I was
             seated at my gilt-edged mirror, busy
             brushing my hair. Self-absorbed, and yet
             I heard the Madder Hat, who told me
             'O Sweetie, yes, your hair wants brushing'
             or was that you who whispered, a palimpsest
             of voices, curiouser and curiouser, obtruding
             worlds within words, like dear Emily's sky
             adrift in a rainbow cortex?

INSTRUCTOR [chalk in hand]: Such ignorance. Time exists.
             It is a system within which we work, but if
             you can't spell 'solipsism' or properly
             define it, where's your proof? As for your
             trite use of the mirror image, I deplore it.
             Clearly a link to your mother's Uncle Ike
             with his refabricating factory in Queens.

BO-PEEP [excited]:   Stop right there! I'm lost!
             Stop with the autobiographical references!

LADY SOLO [brushing]: Anyhow, it was the Bronx. Or Brooklyn.

INSTRUCTOR [irate]:   You were playing at Cassandra. Not being.
             You sat there, eyeing your features, like

        your old antagonist, Arachne, tweaking
        your fingers and cracking all ninety knuckles
        plotting a labyrinth for me, forgetting of
        course—such idiocy, Lord save me—
        that all Hell is divided in threes, like
        all tragedy. If you insist on scrambling your
        centuries ...

LADY SOLO [she instructs]: It was Robertson Davies who said all
        audiences expect a Hero, with whom to be
        subsumed in fatal combat with an, ahem,
        mirror-image Villain, whose antagony

BO-PEEP [she has been trying to take notes on a steno-machine
        but now falls across it, exhausted]: O, Cripes! Now
        you've done it! Antagony! What the
        Anglo-Saxon expletive is that? I was lost
        to begin with, all the way back to Cock
        Robin! I never figured out who killed
        Cock Robin, even when I was young and
        supposedly innocent! And after that, it
        was so irrelevant. Then you throw me
        this Solipsism thing! And a Madder Hat
        as an expert witness! Cripes again!

INSTRUCTOR [murmuring]: 'I,' said the Sparrow. 'With my
        itsy bow and arrow.' Frankly, I suspected
        all that, quasi-automatically, It was pat.
        He's no killer, he's a victim—isn't the Big
        Eye always on him. Enormous feelings
        of guilt by association, grabs for fig leaves
        and it's all trash ...

THE GHOST OF ROBERTSON DAVIES [from behind the mirror]
    I was speaking of medieval morality plays,
    in which Lady Soul was the treasure, always
    in peril, but protected by the Hero ...

LADY SOLO [again, sighing]: Those were indeed the days. It was
    3 a.m. and there was a steady rain, dripping
    on the cartop, and his voice was tired—not
    however, complaining—'You'll want to
    brush your hair again.'

BO-PEEP [she types viciously, snarling]: O shit. O shit. The Fly
    saw him die. With his little eye. That's
    clear enough. And the stupid Fish caught
    his blood, in a little dish. It's all in there.
    It's literal facts from the Coroner's report.
    Why do we have to keep going over and
    over it?

INSTRUCTOR [poorly concealing his giggle]: It's archetypal.
    That's what archetypal means. I never
    believed that Sparrow.

MOTHER GOOSE [*deux ex machina*, she drifts down from the sky]
    I'm here with the proper evidence. You
    want evidence? Well, let me tell you
    Take it from me, dearies, and I'm the
    original Mother, it was those critics.
    The critics did in Cock Robin—called him
    'clever.' That's clearly related to 'cleaver'
    and about as subtle. Ax by swath, that was

no arrow. Better by far, if he'd never
published a word.

LADY SOLO [clearly cannot see Mother Goose, who departs Stage Left with the Instructor]: Maybe what he said was, 'You'll need to brush your hair.'

THE MIRRORED OTHER: What you see reflected here
we can call Drama, or a play. A game of words bumping over others' words. The actors you have seen are simply students, as you may be yourself, someday. The Hero just pretends that he is Robert Browning. [she turns away, with brush uplifted] And when the curtain falls and everybody's gone away, remember. We were all of us pretending. And we have to clear the stage.

THE THREE LITTLE PIGS AND THEIR DIETS

First little piggy tried no-cal zucchini lasagna
with lo-cal pizza and light brews.
But nothing worked.

Second little pig went down the vegetarian path
with occasional fish and chicken, but this porker
harbored and gave in to secret addictions—
slavered after chocolate
and peanut butter
and almond flavored liqueurs.

    The third, alas
grew faint on grapefruit and soda water
while his nemesis, the wolf, of course ...
our wolf—who had an unfortunate, and misspent youth
a wastrel, huffing and puffing with ridiculous exercises to improve
a flaccid musculature—our wolf enriched his coffers, and himself
by writing a series of pig-focused diet books.

Elegant furs our wolf wears now ...
and a sleek, epicurean look.

AN ETERNAL TRIANGLE: HANSEL AND GRETEL AND WHOEVER THAT WAS IN THE KITCHEN

1. Hot Hansel sighs for once upon a time
    the good old days—
    that era of Pre-Knowledge.

    Redreaming the nursery, he seems
    to stand at the hub of wheeling rays of light.
          "That was a time
    before I knew there are no absolutes,"
    he says, and shrugging, pulls up a grin
    like a plastic mask.

2. "Merciful Heaven," cries the older woman.
    "How hot, hot this oven. Yet
    human breath moves through my trees.
    He is remembering, or some new one
    steps through pine shadow.

    Do they never learn?"

3. "I never believed a word my mother said,"
              says Gretel.
    "Entirely as a matter of principle. Never.
    All that stuff about stay out of the woods—
    Don't talk to strangers—It wasn't
    at all what I expected, however—
    I was a tad shocked, in fact."

4. "Gretel was always sharper—she was older—
   one smart cookie," says Hansel, musing.
   "And she moved her hips like dumplings in hot syrup.
   There was a certain supple sweetness ....

   only later, the tart."

5. "My eyes are bad," sighs she by the oven.
   "But I easily calculate degrees of heat, by touch
   and have learned to tell young meat from old this way—
   The young concentrate their heat in lumps—
   the breast, the penis—centers of heat
   but as they age, that heat tends to dissipate
   spreading thin against the growing cold."

6. "I don't know why, I expected incense,"
   Gretel continues. "Attar of ashes of roses ...
   something, certainly more romantic
   than gingerbread ...."

   As she speaks, her hand flutters.
   The bones rise, evident
   like the wing-bones of a bird.
   "The scent was ripe in the air, you know
   thick, like the molasses dark of rich batter ...
   I assumed it was Hansel she was after, of course.
   That dump pup. I should have warned him
   the moment I realized the truth. That scent
   was more the velour of an old Ford's back-seat—lust
   oozed in, and a portion of dust.
         I was sweating. I was
   you see, ashamed."

7. "She was awfully attractive, in basic black,"
Hansel recalls, wistful "Veiled in shadows ...
and slim. Not like my silly, plumpish sister
though God knows, I've followed Gretel
fawning, through many a woods
and would again, God help me, forever.

    But the old girl wouldn't
give me a tumble. No. It was all for Gretel."
He pouts, uneasy. "All for Sissy Gretel.
Yet I dream of her sharp teeth
and hunger ... and have this
creepy feeling —
somewhere, she waits.

THE VINE FABLE

A perverse young woman of our village was told many many times never to eat the seeds of watermelons: don't suck them, don't chew them, don't mess around, or you will be in big, fat trouble. All the old women agreed. Nothing good can come from eating watermelon seeds.

Perversely, the girl didn't listen. After one particularly sweet-meloned summer, it was seen in the fall and winter months that her belly had blossomed. "Oho!" cackled the old women, shaking their arthritic fingers, "Didn't we tell you? We warned you! See what happens when you don't listen!"

As usual, the perverse young woman ignored the old biddies. She smiled maternally, and was often seen to pat or caress her burgeoning belly. "Mmm," she murmured. "O, Sweetness, they did try to warn me. But aren't we glad ...."

Her condition was monitored by everyone in the village—even our Idiot took notes. As she neared her delivery, long green vines coiled delicately from the hem of her skirt, and verdant tendrils looped gently about her knees. "See! See!" shrieked the old women. "Watermelon! Don't we warn ALL young women? Don't we try!"

At length, the young woman was delivered. The fruits of her labor—if you'll pardon my putting it that way—were two musk melons and a small cantaloupe. "It's a wise woman who knows the father of her produce," she snickered, winking. "And as for produce, those old women don't know beans."

YOU'RE QUITE SURE THEN, THAT YOU HAVE GROWN UP?

Here's a rap for your knuckles, I'd like, Lady of the Ruler
to try: teach me scales up strange ladders, C D and make me cry
"You're an odd thoughty child, but you don't fool me. I
have been worried by experts. Lightly! Lightly! The wrists
should think of flowers." (Bleeding-Heart. Jump-Up. Hemlock.)
"You are D-I-F-F-E-R-E-N-T from the others. Not P-R-E-T-T-Y."

"No one is to leave this room without permission. Clear?
T. As in Telephone." (Momma twists the wire, calling Nanny
"You're the only one left that I can talk to." Tell Nanny
who drew on the wall with blue crayola?") Tasted like tunafish
and Daddy's beer. Trees are blurs like green ogre's ears.
D. is a long line with a belly. B, double belly. P, a head.

Yes, I said, I said I didn't do it. The Righteous are rewarded
who they are, but Sinners be cast down. Down. Step on a crack
and be zapped, like that, without even stopping for dinner.
Light up like a lamp, and die. Milkweed juice is also poison.
And white lumps in bacon, that will not fry. Slap, and down
flies the ruler, from Heaven. D.E.F. The quiet sky.

CINDERELLA SAID TO HER UGLY STEPSISTER

To your credit, you always have
flaunted your ugliness, hap
humming hap stuck your chin out
happily, with all its warts
slept with sweeps and oystermen

I respect your honesty, ever

I myself not always frank, sat
quietly in my corner, circumspect
hum humble trimming my toenails
behaved with discretion, yet
dreamed of orgies, happily ever

I admit it now, humming hap hap

don't say my Prince's charming eyes
are crossed, happily happily or
ever mention halitosis, aft
in the same breath, hap
happily. It's too like sour grapes

it does not become you. Ever after.

THE CHASED: A RE-VISION

Queer greed, seen backwards
over the shoulder, or mirrored—that thirst
for moments, colors, shapes of words
hones my fingers, adz-wise, as I reach
through hedgerows, like Cinderella
fleeing shadows.

I suppose
opened—either of us—there'd be
no stomach to us, only clockworks
coiled and wound, fine
for digesting symbols, vision
        works of escape ...

    At sea
  rain hangs down
  whisking the horizon, and gulls
  fly with their heads cocked, watching
      the weather colors, expectant
  and the sails
  bellied, curve together
  worry against the wind
  as the ticking of water against the hull
      presumes the shore—
  slate-grey water
  puckering under sudden rain.

But I sail hot, sail cold, depending

not on externals, but on that queer greed
driving, from sea to street
         on to dark hedgerows
shadowed alleys, like a creature
chased, like Cinderella
shoes in hand.

I like this.
And more's the pity. My fool laugh
follows, clacking in privet hedges
as I run, grabbing stuff of shadows   'til the clock
         strikes midnight: the dial fingers
clap together—scissor blades
that snap shut, like Fates.

But wait. Tick's proclivity
is chasing Tock. This opens up
a further moment of the tattered race—
magic ravels of the skein.

Wayne Hogan

UNCLE IKE, MOVER AND SHAPER

paid for the family
steerage, from Vilna
Mom said, someplace Polish
came over first and made much gelt
from old mirrors, old x-ray plates
        melted them down
    his magic touch
recovering silver—

a rich man, Mom said
she didn't love him much, but
loved to visit his factory, to see
those boxes of mirror shards
waiting; sliced her leg one time—
that never stopped her—that's
a scar she has, today.

    Me, I never knew him
never hardly knew he lurked there
back in our history—shaper
and mover—bequeathing me
cracked images for poems
dozens of doubled faces
to crop up, from deep
where my dreams are.

Two Mother Poems

GERTRUDE'S GARDEN—(IT'S ALSO MY UPSTART MOTHER'S NAME)

p rose is a rose rose rose rose rose rose ro

up rose rose rose rose rose rose rose rose

rose rose rose LIVERWORT rose rose ro

up rose rose rose rose rose rose rose rose

p rose is a rose rose rose rose rose is a ro

UP BUTTERCUP rose rose rose rose up

FOUND POEM: MY MOTHER, THE TYPIST, PRACTICES AFTER THE STROKE

                nnnnnnnnnnnnnnnnnnnnnn
        This is the way to go home wouldn't
you say so/ Thank you very much for doing the ribbon for me
Ruth. Do hope the carpenters have done a good job for you
Ruthie. Will you let me know how you made out with them.
This has been a very good day so far. may it continue.
Thank you for being able to go to the bank and get everything
done. Thank you for letting me be able to type. Amen. amen.
halelujah. This is the way to type an answer to Ceci's letter
don't you think? I do-- our's not to reason why, ours to do
and die. Yes I think that is very good what do you think
Ruthie? this is Sunday morning and I am going to try and
answer some letters. Bravo!

FLYING TO GATWICK, SHE DRIFTS BACK WITH A NEW BOOK OF POEMS

> ... *'Make room*
> *for the roots!' my mother cries,*
>   *'Dig the hole deeper.'*
>   Stanley Kunitz, "My Mother's Pears"

O, I was never so glad to find a book in an
airport, though O, the money passed
in Atlanta bookstores is
beyond remembrance. This book I knew, before
I'd touched it: its heft a known proposition.
O, I said to myself, doesn't this have—and it does.
                     His pear poem!

a poem to cherish, makes this book
worth (that which is without cost) priceless

not to be confused with worthless, which would be
more like today's horoscope for Aquarius:

> *you will meet an old friend; you*
> *will enjoy reminiscing.*

the words hop in my head: all my old friends are dead.
Which ghosts then, does that Zodiac prefigure?

                Sure enough,
here's Glenda stepping forward, a slim blonde
who hauls a paisley overnighter ever closer—
but she's way too busty. Not to mention, she's living.

This book, however
holds for me an old friend poem.
Like the water-carrier, it pours its words
as out of a bucket, liquescent sound, the poet's blood

as if over a knifeblade. Once
up in Worcester, a tourbus driver read us this poem
while in the bus windows, pear tree branches, yellowing
in the late summer sun, swayed, uplifted ...
his mother's pear tree now holds an angel. (Indoors
we ate chocolate chip cookies and sipped lemonade politely)
Someone's stuck a white angel up, crooked, where the tree forks
growing—and I was hearing my mother again, saying

almost off-handed: "Never be afraid.
You have good roots. You come
from excellent blood."

PART TWO:
OF THE CLASSROOM, AND THE HOUSE

LEDA, IN THE CLASSROOM

can count on her fingers
realistic, trochee cadences
and the repetition of symbols:

    to "perne in a gyre"
she explains, is to balance
on that spiral staircase

listening again
for the rustle of feathers—

as the heart swarms upwards
urgent, the mind
seeks past discretion, dazed.

ON THE WAY

For C.

between faculty meeting
and the post office, I heard you say:
Laugh. It's better than crying.

Someone else spoke
a rattle of attendance figures, then
later, additions of postage

and even later, between
the beach and grocery shopping
again you told me: Laugh.

The sand, sunwarmed
was so like you, when I turned—
the leftover sun, on lobes of sand

when I turned onto mybelly
felt so like your body
it didn't matter that the sky

had gone. On the way
between living and dying
I heard you. You were crying.

SHE STEALS A METAPHOR
FROM SYLVIA PLATH'S POEM ABOUT A GOOSE

While I eat grits
she fattens on the finest grain.

and here's ourselves, dichotomous again
in one gaunt goose long doomed
for strutting childless through a Disney world—
whose raddled chins proclaim
eternal possibility. Those empty eggs of dream
(yolk golden) some second self has spun
of words, of a diet of ghost grain, husks
and chaff, of no-cal syllables ...
the avarice in Rumplestiltskin's name.

But how we fed her: bits and snips of all the best
'til she led the gaggle; outshone, at least
her struggling sisters and their gosling broods.
In spite of this, or yes
more like because of it, the knife waits
honed and inevitable. Her blood's foreknown
with all the rest—the staple grin
that oversees the final, web-thin slice
to leak that life in steamy lust—
the execution of the final line.

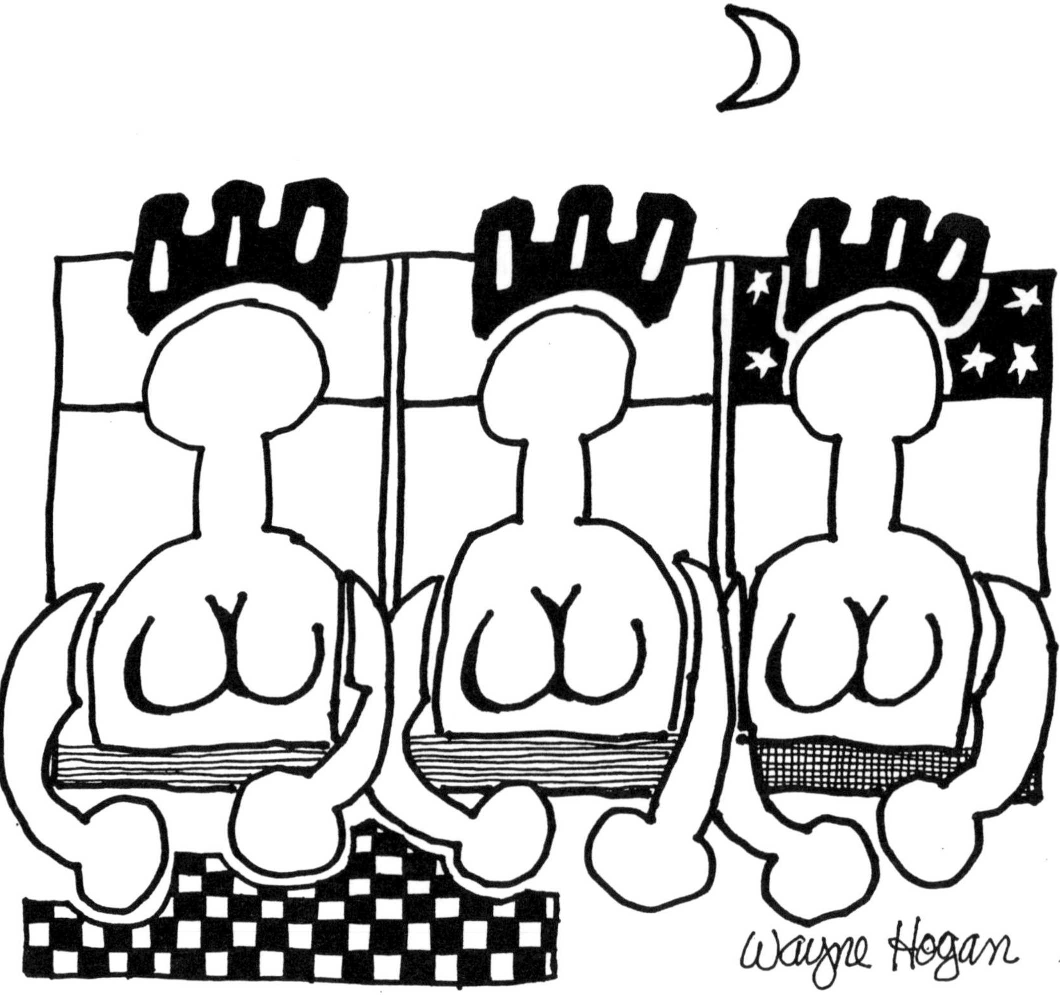
Wayne Hogan

WATCHING A MOVIE AND WRITING A POEM

1.

A sign says MANUFACTURY? What was it
I said today? Is there any such word as
O I wish I remembered
Whose funeral is this, anyway? Women
the stucco peels away from old brick—
                  there is a Spanish poem
by Jorge Manrique, *Coplas*, on the death
of his father—they look like olive trees
gripping the mountain, the taut blue sky

It was a very good word for using

and I wish I hadn't forgotten.
All life is transitory, heading like rivers
to a sea called Death

and I'd thought about people in general, wide
smiling people; foolish to forget, easy

2.

over the years, his grief remains
        (Jorge Manrique's)
call it *ubi sunt*? or *adonde van*? Gone.
He writes of silver-bordered skirts, mirrors
helmets, scents
      the past registered

forgets to add he will be leaving too
like the word I made up today / erased

     A woman carries a basket

bread / yeast is a thing goes on and on
baking to baking, the thrifty wife saves
for the next day's batch, a wad of leaven
always. Funny, but Jorge Manrique'
               never writes of food
only of gold, vanished glory, and lust

But after funerals
       there were always women
carrying baskets. Fresh-baked bread.

SLIDES: ROOM 6C, DR. DOBROVSKY'S SUMMER VACATION
CORK TREES IN SALAMANCA [Actually Possibly Seville]

I must confess my mind wanders
The elderly people in Paris are merely background
an old woman with [*lapis lazuli*] mignonettes to sell
and banks of citron yellow jonquils in rusted cans; the old
man who plays the accordion; violet light of sun in rain

is like Murillo, or Renoir, Impressionist
but Lautrec's lights are strictly glare; this is soft
and biologically speaking the daffodil is *Narcissus pseudo-*
narcissus (where are we here?) linguistically, kin
to Middle English affodille, Latin doublet of Asphodel
and I have never been to Paris, but here we are, very young

the air damp with scents of rain and jonquils
we must have met here this afternoon, seeking shelter
cups of absinthe, that was a young thing to drink then
"saucers," they called them, at the Divon Japonais, Jane Avril
sat at the bar in black, down to her cuckoo ostrich feathers
sitting by Eduard, listening to Evette, 75 *Rue des Martyrs*
(Toulouse caught her)

                      black and white and red his register
and I have missed how we arrived at these cypress trees
mouldering grey walls that drip, with lavender hills beyond
birds only guessed at. There must be little birds here
swarming in the sunlit branches. We met in Paris?
Murillo died in 1682, and was therefore not
definitely no Impressionist

So. We met in Paris, drove to Spain in the rented Simca
pretending to be friends of Hemingway, talking of Papa, who
understood wine in furry bottles; drove on to Salamanca
because it has a pretty name, ignoring the bulls, the daisies
until here. We've arrived at the cork trees in flower
and the Moorish gardens, driving sharp-turned roads
                        up into the mountains. There will be rain

thunder behind us rolls out like dice
(throughout his life, Toulouse-Lautrec never lost interest
in women, horses, or the circus) Hemingway dead too
since Lord, the hills of Idaho (somebody answer that damned
telephone) and I can see how your hand
brushes my raveled sweater, how you grip my arm, you are saying

how it always ends, and you're right. We are in bed.

The cork trees, better known in some circles
as the oak, *alcorque*—you are laughing
we have slid together, clean and young again
"And then," says Dr. Dobrovsky, "We went on to Xerex
famous for its wineries, and crossword puzzles"
and every story beginning in Paris should end
         with Spanish wine, beside the bed.

LOOKING UP "ECPYROSIS"

For Young Z, after his triple by-pass

"In the formal, discursive mode," she said
dreaming crepuscular spiders, eaten by flame—
an overlapped image from the classroom, sloppy.
"Now when Robert Lowell sees the same
                Jonathan Edwards' spiders ..."
assumes no one is listening, webs, loops, a cord
limpid, of words in the flickering moment
"... he is working from a fine family tradition
           of course."

Notices again how winter sunlight caught
in his cigarettes' cellophane—not Lowell's
though stolid Amy appears, with cigar, tapping
ash, marking meters—"A well-known family
like the Mathers or the Cottons, the Edwards
had sons expected to excel, who stuttered, or
sometimes had visions, spiders imploding
           in flame."

Only later comes that wonder
like a reek of tobacco wisp, did they catch
that careful wording, that hinted connection
vision on vision, the families poetic
seething in rubric-red flame—implosion here
as opposed to ecpyrosis—a burn
from the heart-core outward—this year's
in-moving Hell, too close to home.

LOOKING FOR KIERKEGAARD IN A STRANGE NOVEL

an essence perhaps, that begins
and ends on paper, or a box
rosewood, warped, long buried

with candle-ends and bits of string—
there were letters, wrapped in red
shreds of a made-up diary

    (stutterings of a bride
or possibly a prostitute, some
human otherness to perceive—or
philosophies of loving)

               we'd looked
over a mermaid's shoulder
into a lust for sea-death, lost.

It ended more like a fable
with the opening of Pandora's box.
It begins and ends with paper

as if there could be paper seeds.

THURSDAY'S POEM

Tomorrow is my day to read all day in Spanish
Manana, and the days slip by ...
the old dog ages, kept alive on aspirin
                            and love
stands, back knees bent for balance
or a leap to Heaven, her blind eyes showing
                          too many whys.

Tomorrow is my day to study Spanish
manana, Spanish is the loving tongue ...
and I remember how his shirt felt
                        but not his lips

       yes, lips
but more, warm fabric.
The old dog has no appetite, and the young one
slavers after
hound dog days.

Tomorrow is my day for Spanish.
Manana, and then after say, the moon rises
      an old dog can't tell night from day
      so we walk the beach all hours
                    me leading
    the seeing eye, dreaming
in bad Spanish, leading her into gorse
the dune brush—*te quiero*, the Spanish
make no distinction, much
between lust and love. The lucid Spanish
say I will be yours, God willing
tomorrow, or some day.

THE OLD DOG

Koko says
the ocean is
   just water

    &

Koko says
poems are just
   words

    &

Koko being
fifteen
senile
& half blind

  still

she has a nice
way of
looking at
   things

especially
the morning sun
   (blinking)
      O yes
still here

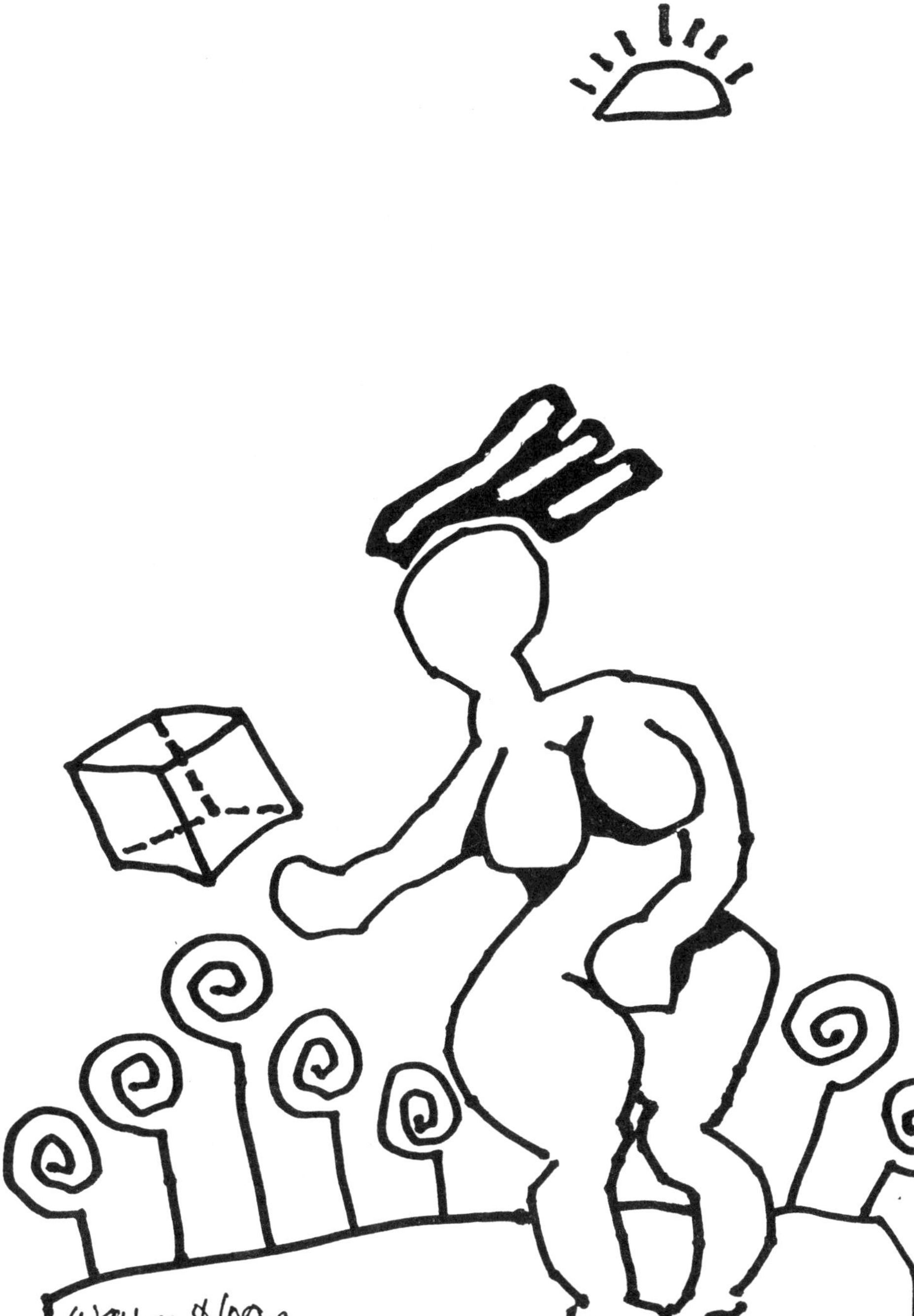
Wayne Hogan

MOMENT APOCALYPTIC: WITH BUBBA, A GERMAN SHEPHERD, AND A BLUEFISH

Tomorrow, I said, will be another anomaly
but somehow sunnier, when if ever I can finish this
because the aluminum spoon, on plastic scales
goes awkward
the scales bend over, fly down to the floor—
fish scales, though I dream a concertina, mellow—
it was supposed to be cool and cloudy, a northeaster
weather like music, a vast poetic concerto
best forgotten. I tell you, Bubba, it's apocalyptic
how I keep mislaying my epigrams, Ferlinghetti
                all those people
and you don't know an epigram from Jesus, do you?

I'd forgotten how bluefish flesh turns blue again
like surf water under west wind, under the faucet—
the cold water, tapped, flows cold
and the white ribbed fishmeat turns blue-green—
it's an interior rainbow, with peacock feathering
ripples. "Poets are litmus paper." That was it.
Someone said it. "They test the acidity of our days
and the sourness of their generations."
                      But I always forget
is it pink or blue, for acid? State of my mind:
amazed. How the flesh held under water turns blue-
        green—a living wetness
and the guts are blood brown, pollen yellow.
Tomorrow may bring another mental trauma, Bubba.
Some other half-caught memory slip off the hook.
                    And there that head sits, mauve eyes
filmed for swimming; seeping life fluids
into yesterday's newsprint—looking out at us, today.

FROM THE TUB, SHE TEACHES HER GERMAN SHEPHERD, BUBBA A LESSON OF TONGUES & TABOOS

no mange vous pas
is dumb half French from somewhere
manger being to eat when I meant *comer*
no coma I meant to say do not eat
the soap, *el jabon* damnit *se permite*:
es defendu is a DON'T DO THAT.
Do Not Eat the Soap. Especially You
with the delicate nervous digestive system
                                  Sweet Jesus
(*Jesu Cristo*) licking bubbles from my arm
is also a NO in all the tongues *Non et* Nope
et cetera. Thus we defend our *virtu*
you know. Sorry. Erase that.
When I say "Yes okay, you know," I know
I am confusing you, "k-n-o-w" being "no"
so what's the use. *No eaty vous pas
la sopa*—I said soup now, isn't good for you
                                  either
ni jabon ni sopa de jabon: soap soup
jamon, however, the hambone
you not being kosher Jewish it's okay—
huesos de jamon or Catholic on Friday
no hambones, no *jamon y huevos*, no *huevos*
since eggs make you sick too, *fritos* or
any other way. *El estomago* whoopsy.
You remember? *No vamos* a vomit today.

WHAT LOLA—A DOG BROUGHT UP
ON WALLACE STEVENS—

   hears: a pleasant kerchunk
of the refrigerator, whose door closes;

the click of claws on dew-wet grass
when the neighbors' pied cat comes

crouching, teasing; the clackle, clackle, clackle of the bike
that bastard kid rides;

nothing I say
except, maybe, if I whisper
"cookie," she'll cock (intently) her eye.

THE INVENTORY QUEEN

Elegant in dungarees of green, she enters, murmuring
obscenities of greeting to the drooping cockatiel;
speaks with quick tongue of celery seed.

The night's "night-blue ... an inconstant thing."
Dogs sleep, with the click-clack of attic mice obscured
by the drip of plumbing. Can this be

stuff of art? The "fiction of an absolute"? She doubts it.
But what remains when love has blurred
from flame to ash, by embers? My "fluent mundo," listen.

We will confound the moon with imagery: a vast
descriptive catalogue (as fate will have it) of trash
caught in the falling of a beam of sight from a. to b.

Enter: a. [east wall, top-most shelf] assorted journals
non-continuous, from youth to now, sporadic. Those three
spiral-bound are one strange year, unpaginated.

b. one wooden pseudo-Nutcracker, green uniform and gun.
Assorted clowns. Erratum here. Sub-lists are needed.
Clown with yo-yo. Clown with trumpet. Barefoot clown

with beach ball. c. small mouse, with tambourine.
d. [on wall] a card of Sigmund Freud, in caricature
to keep us straight and narrow. The Blue Guitar

Picasso—tilted on its tack—blue man with tan guitar
blushed blue. She loses track, in shadow. Dragons emerge

with rick-rack spinal trimming: "this 'hoard / of
            destructions'"

and "Things as they are." A rattaned sangria jar's above
photo of John Donne, in shroud; other belated greetings—
light that tumbles out of stars, and final clowns, who soar

on thin gilt webbing. She speaks: "It's surely time for Z?"
and regal, jots the final entry: z. one blue steel box
guaranteed to last through fire, flood or holocaust.

Unlocked, it holds beneath a skin of dust
invalid credit cards, a copy of divorce decree—
held safe forever. "Ridiculous."

The cockatiel awakes to cackle "Celery, celery seed."
They neither catch the gist of what each means, nor
sense the blueness of their sudden music.

ONCE, WHEN I WAS ESTHER WILLIAMS

    we went to Apu-someplace I can't spell
South American, *el sur*, the water so blue
tan azul, you couldn't spill it
       and Jose Somebody was playing
piano, Iturbi, and O it was lovely

      we all had to cry a little
         so it would look like living
     later on he got stump legs
being what'shis name the poster painter
no: that was somebody longer legs, Ferrar
       trotting up Montemarte
      on bentover ankles, absinthed
        but I was myself
Edith Piaf by then

      O yes, *si*, *oui*, yes
         singing and weeping chiffon

it was only after then
     in spite of all the ex-everybodies
         in the end
I learned to keep my mouth shut. About
     anything real. Just hum.

PRESUMING ON EMILY'S #341

After great Crisis, come a gentler Time—
The Heart slumps, quiet, like soft Ice Cream
Relaxed into its Cone—The Nerves, unharried
Question what to do? and dumb

The Fingers move, methodical, for Chores—
Of cleaning out—
A Lysol Air
Asepsis known—
The corners of refrigerated Drawers.

This is the Moment of the Mushroom Spoor—
Remembered, if yet known—
The Lettuce Slush, the half-gnawed Bone—
First—Slop—then Bag it—Let it go.

BEGINNING HER CLEARLY MAD, UNFINISHED JOURNAL OF HOROSCOPERY AND DREAMS

1/1

New ideas ... can be useful. Be
businesslike in your activities.
Cooperation will be easier to obtain.

Dear Sir: in re yrs of last Dec 6 please
contact again, please ans communicate
saw sparrows yesterday taking a bath
                in muddy water
dogs dug a hole & up came water
            garbled
reminded me of Friday in the gardens.
           No new idea
              Eden, a golf course in
Dear Sir: yr attendance most desired at
private party at the Gates, Huns &
Barbarians gathered in Times Square, saw
              Time descend aglitter
                in a multipolygonal Apple
but here not enof for a quorum, ever
Food is important, so is praying
blushed Monday when you remarked
              my temperature
must be 1000002 degrees, moved soft
like Sir Cedric in his copper armor
gentle remembrance of evil
but yrs of anno domini, rec'd.

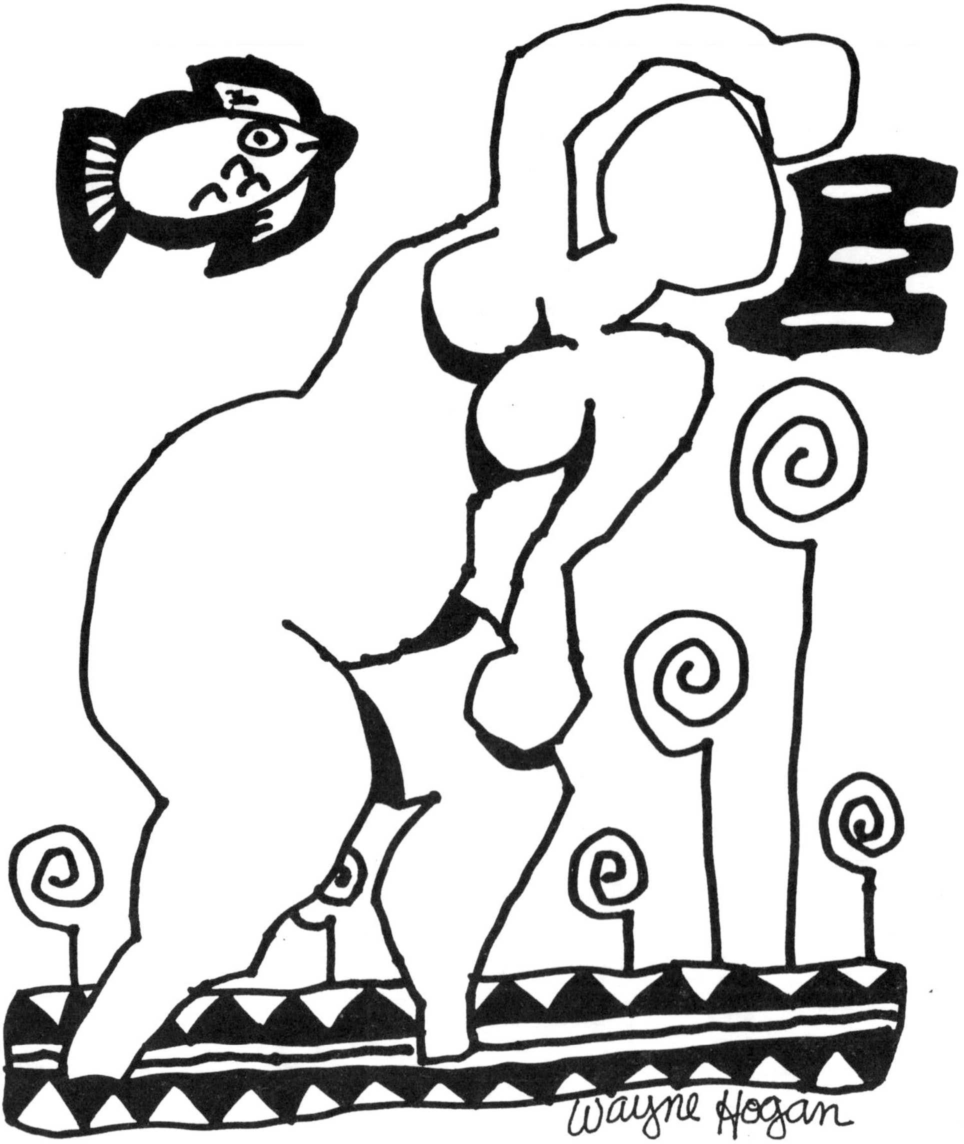
Wayne Hogan

1/2

*Disquieting: Attention to your health
and to very personal problems will be ...
useful.*

probably.
Questions I had mostly concerned a clothespin
dropped this a m into the ivy, old leaves
dust of old snows, and never found it
but the search was—how to say this?
a finding of what there is nice, about ivy
how it dangles pale roots on frozen clods
frost icing on leather, crackle leaved
succulent quivering / trying to hang pillows
in the one day's sun. Crack in my shoulder
predicting rain / more rain / arm in a sling
looked for a clothespin couldn't find it
realized I didn't talk to anyone all day
                       but dogs
told them we'd have stew again.

1/3

*Someone in the background may offer ...
information*

up at 2 a m reading Dos Passos'
first novel, initiation, surprising how conventional
        thinking however he started out
where he needed to be, using people
        he knew he needed
the French teacher fishing in a stream
        spectacles, the water roiled
        by Fiats being washed by
        volunteers, upstream
naive, he says, but looking
didn't fall into fabricated whitetoothed heroes
didn't diddle fictive invention
        looked
over the scene / people and dreams

some never see their own dreaming
fall off, right at the last minute
no guts at the crest, and a fear to maybe see

wondered myself did I travel 400 miles
        north, arm in a sling
just to gather my courage, write you
        one line
a true question
(business like) do you remember rain?

TWO GOOD BITCH POEMS

1. First Poem For Kalliope Jane
   The Basset-Beagle Pup

Jane, Jane
you've
doodled away your walk
             again.
You haven't done this
though you've
snuffled at that

    and I, alas
am only a fat
black shadow, that
    ends with pale toes
in the grass.

2. Short Poem For Lily Belly
   A Tall Tan German Shepherd

Dog, O good old dog
what I like is

open the door for you
and coming in there

from sunlight
you bring sunwarmth in your hair.

LISTENING TO YOUR SONG, STUDYING

Karl Marx was today's schedule, and I didn't
only as far as Hegel, and the Ideal

George Gershwin, you idiot, I was tired or lazy, wanting
rhapsodic, like the soundtrack of *Zhivago* ....
hi-fi is the opiate of the people, stereo twice as, O Love
pyrotechnique (poems) but you don't like them all

                so I wonder which words
now, dialectic for tomorrow. There is a God
and a Hell, too. I hold it. Across the hand you touched
the dead winds blow
        kisses on my lovelines.

Someone keeps score. Tree sun sifts through a window
and I am, as always, yours.

PART THREE: OF TRAVELS, FIELD TRIPS TAKEN OR DREAMED

LOOKING FOR D.H. LAWRENCE, IN TAORMINA

found him, or his spirit, in all those flowers
colors, anthers, kazillion petals
orchards full of acid citrus, twisted olives ...

chased him, up those tiered alleys
steep-stepped up to azure sky-blue, white-washed
old walls hung with bougainvillea ....

found him, all those people, dusky, bright-eyed
looking for bargains, looking for outdoor
cappuccino under bright umbrellas
looking for love.

SHE INTERVIEWS D.H. LAWRENCE
NOT EITHER IN HEAVEN NOR IN HELL, BUT

somewhere between illness and equilibrium—

Q: The suffering of your mother was
DHL: in part responsible for an interest in
                rabbits, the quest
       Etruscans, the vast dark cypresses
Q: but what accounts for your acceptance of
DHL: displacement and exile? perhaps an idea
       strangers are not asked impertinent questions—
       no why did you spend so much on a ticket to joy
            you could have had cheaper on Wednesday—
       show that wound here, that scar there, undercuts
Q: and is there always the thirst? the need to call
            or reach out to the Other?
DHL: half of oneself, the not quite
            contactable? So far as I know.

KIOSK AND GAZEBO: A DUO

1. KIOSK / MIASMA

"Cool shoes, Dude," says the tall man.

His emaciated friend has eaten halfway into a hotdog; there is piccalilli in his moustache. He nods, chewing.

I don't like the looks of either one. I wish another woman would enter. There is a huddled person in back of the kiosk, but sexless, certainly not helpful. It occurs to me I'm wishing for my mother. But she would never come to such a place.

Warm rain tosses noisy drops against the back wall and roof, making a petulant clamor. I decide that when the bus arrives, if it ever does, I will wait here; perhaps better companions will arrive. That's flimsy thinking, and I know it—I blame the kiosk's swampy air, the rain.

The bus comes rumbling out of the wet darkness. The sign above the driver reads: SNAKE EYES.

What kind of destination is .... Before I finish the question, the driver reaches up and cranks a knob. The sign changes: TIME

2. GAZEBO / OZONE

"You've been ill," says Edgar Allan Poe, gazing at me from the weather-beaten rail. "I know the feeling."

The air is chill and I wonder why they put me out here in my cocoon of blankets. It may be to offset the fever. There is a clock beneath my couch, and as it ticks I rather think the sound is from a spider, cracking its knuckles. I wish he would say something else. I would like an epiphany. A revelation. How did he die, really? Something informative might make my reputation.

He comes near and holds out a book. I read the spidery writing: "the fact, that deed, the thing *diddling* is somewhat difficult to define." I think what comes after is a definition of "minute," as in "small." Small scale.

If I had a pencil with me, I decide, I would write a haiku right this minute. I would steal an image from who was that? something I was reading before all this, in which the stems of certain plants were seen as insect legs, tottering in a swamp. That is, if I had any paper.

Very tall mosquitoes require a warmer climate. Here, the air is biting, crisp. It's something about biting, at that, that I want to discuss with Poe, but he takes the pages away, nodding. I see traces of piccalilli in the fringe of his moth-eaten moustache.

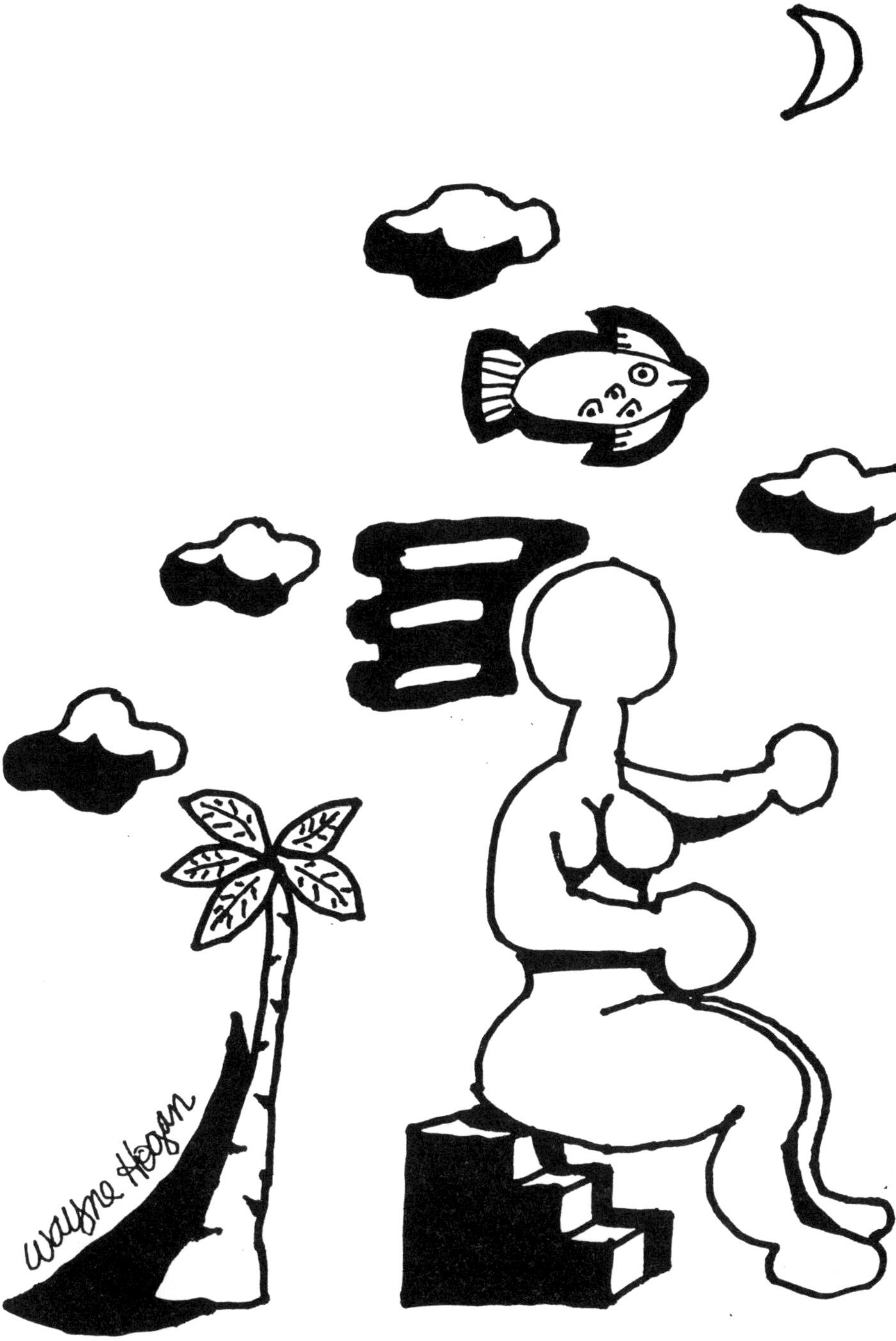
Wayne Hogan

UNOFFICIAL LOG: *S.S. ORIZABA*, APRIL 26, 1932

04:35   Restless. Watched Cookie heave trash
over the aft rail, making a wake of melon rinds and eggshells—
a thrash of shark fins attacking the scavengers
attacking orange peels—vegetable matter attracts
this strange crowd, this action
then they vanish.

10:30   Received reports on the missing passenger—
over the rail, just sauntered up one witness says, yes
as suspected, this was the same man in earlier reports
who instigated that riot, was beaten up—advances
made to the pale young steward, a first class
trouble maker—a poet

younger than he looked by this. One would have thought
seeing his face, he was an old man. Took with him
notes for an epic—they say—a saga
of Aztec or Inca conquest.
    No survivors there, either.

15:30   Spotted the pale young steward, lithe
as he filched a gardenia from the Captain's table—white
as a star, a small flower he took and tossed overboard
over the aft rail—white star into cobalt water.
Heard his shout—This is for the bells you rang
in Taxco, to break the morning. This is for
    the Saint whose day you honored."

It may (eventually) wash ashore.

THOUGH PAGAN AT HEART, SHE CELEBRATES THE FEAST OF MARY MAGDALENE

Centuries later, still, I'd celebrate this sister—
the comfortable woman—

a woman to appreciate, lonely
in spite of, or because of

all those husbands, reportedly not hers.
I've seen how the Old Masters picture this Mary

tall, the face sad, leaning lissome at a well
but that's not how I see her. It's not easy

being a comfort to husbands; not ever easy
on a body. One's crippled early.

There's arthritis to gnarl the hands
that once gave pleasure, other

afflictions. One becomes nearsighted—
they say she mistook Christ for the gardener—

told him, trembling, go away Gardener—Let me
tend to the body, even when no one else will;

let me care for my friend, my teacher
in death as in life, in life though crossed in death.

Christ Church, Oxford, July 22, 1998

IN REAL LIFE, AS IN THE THEATRE

of scotch, one runs across so many humbugs, if
you know what I for instance was hearing the other
day this gentleman from Scotland, speaking of
Glenlivet was quite emphatic, King George IV in 1822
drank nothing else. Gorse bristled in my mind, and
what is it? heath. no. broom. yellow. The heath
was black and the busdriver said come back in August
when it's lavender and lovely, lass. Lavender is
the South, Renoir and picnics. Yes. A bottle was
brought up from the cellar and pressed into the
hands of King George IV. Lord Coryingham, the
Chamberlain, had been frantic. Ah. He drinks and
nods. The wind blows briskly through the sedges.
In the liquid, limber, amber, is the scent of peat.

READING ABOUT BOSWELL'S CLAP, IN EDINBURGH LATELY ARRIVED BY BUS FROM LONDON

*With Boswell words were everything. Promiscuity ...
had an ugly sound in his ear, but concubinage was Biblical.*
   William B. Ober, M.D., *"Boswell's Clap"*

    It's juxtaposed: the desert rock and grit religion
in a mind raised up in this country lasciviously green.
Here, it's spring. Earlier passing through Wordsworth country
there were daffodils—thousands of bulbs planted by the poet
in memory of Dorothy? or his daughter?—imagine small, sad
William in his black frock coat, down on his knees, digging.
Those roots go deep. And here the golden bushes we see
bouncing past the windows (of course, another illusion)
are "gorse, better known as broom, hereabouts," the driver
a mine of information—but he didn't know for sure about
Wordsworth—he says "The black you see is the heather ...
Come back, see it in August, you'll weep for it, Darlin', for
the beauty of it. It's all a matter of bein' in the right place,
with the right coins, and time."
    Boswell's bus, I read, was a post-chaise, to help avoid
the bumpier coach ride, taking the mercury for his cure, and
the rides to London. He'd have seen the same broom, golden
in the hills; the sheep, with those white dit-dot balls, grazing
in the lush green—"Those are rutabagas, Darlin'. They roll
them down like bowling balls, feed for the lambs and mothers."
A woman on the bus, Maria, from Buenos Aires, sought
all morning for the right word for "Homesick"—she had this
feeling she called a *"tristesse,"* a longing for a loved one, and
for a decent cup of coffee. Not *"Tey-Cha,"* the tea-coffee
of the British—hers, bi-lingual gifts, untranslatable griefs.

Later (it's always later) I thought of the Spanish word
"*crepuscularia*" ... a peculiar sadness of twilight, with a scent
as of purled crepe myrtle, or iodine of a remembered beach.
Boswell also bumped along the highway, tourist, seeking
relief, and the right word to apply to his damnation.

    A twisted baggage, words and memories: like
"Raddle-saddle." The driver winked and told us why sheep
we saw were splotched different colors—some on the rear
and others on the shoulder. "That's the farmer's doin', Darlin'.
Shoulder marks are the grade marks. If a ewe's been good—
if she's had twins, say—they daub her a red mark, to save.
But if she only had one, or is aging, a blue daub marks her
down for slaughter. This handy device—the raddle-saddle's
a harness on the ram, with a pouch of dye—that's the way
they'll rate the rams. It's a cinch. If he hits on a ewe, she's
marked with his color, all winter. He must mark enough
ewes, then, to save his own life."

    We, tourists of the desert religion, are heard to snicker.
But it's odd, the juxtaposition—a "*tristesse*," Boswell
and his killing disease, spring and the sensual sheep—
it's August and heather, that make one cry.

WAYSIDE FLOWERS, WELL

First there were fist-sized
lotus, gasping
in the murk, pond
at the obsessive artist's
(he more interested
in 13th Century tiles
        than in how
his lilies groped
for a living)
        but then
at St. Winifred's Well, in
Woolston, Shropshire
where we almost fell in
laughing, there were
        yellows
(Chris said, "Surely
that's celandine") tiny
yellow poppies
in a maze, amazing, well—
those waters are supposed
by the local gentry
to cure lameness—dark
waters, curding up
        (Winifred's bones
rested here, they say, on
their sacred journey) but
there was such laughter
        about the words
"Flower," like "plougher"
and "Flow-er," the Well

O, O, the Well flows
            lovely
                gives root-room
in treacherous slime
among well-stones, to
the tiny shining stars
the celandine.

IN RENOIR'S DINING ROOM
AT *LES COLLETTES*

(with Tim Tubbs)

when I asked where
is the kitchen?
having earlier found
kitchens of interest
Tim said: Think
of what was.

The sun streamed
up from the sea
up from Cagnes-sur-mer
reflected from slates
and off olive leaves
bringing visions—

scrambled eggs and bacon
(that thick ham-slice
bacon of Europeans) with
croissants, raspberries—
the kitchen? would be
outside, an outhouse—

prim housemaids, bow aprons
brought in the breakfast
in to this sunlight.
It was, we agree
a different circumstance
a different age. But O
O, this clear light.
O, this day.

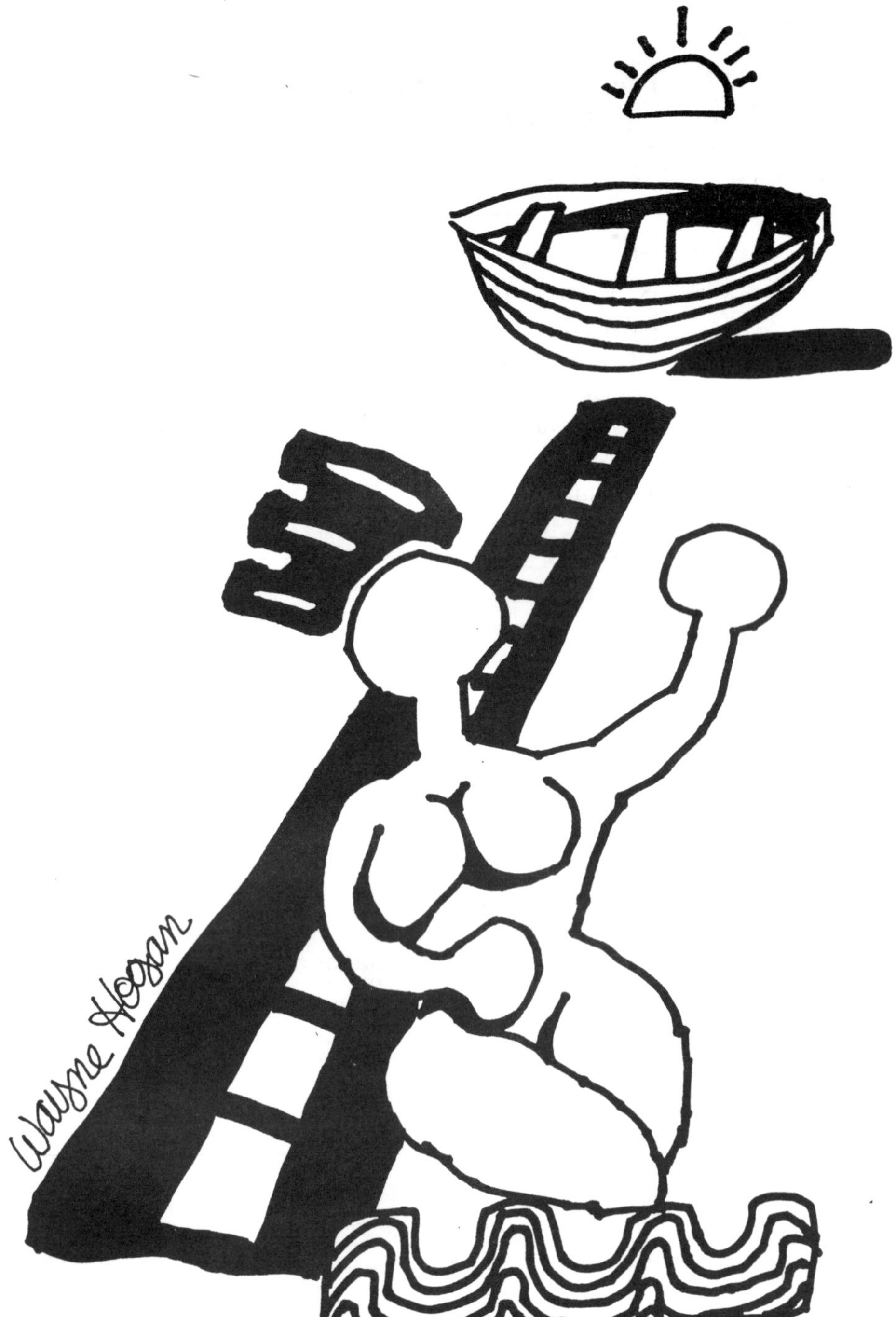
Wayne Hogan

HER MATISSE NOTES ....

in Vence, well I went to Vence looking for some sign of
D.H. Lawrence who died there and has been forgotten
but if the hotel of Henri Matisse had been open, perhaps
that would have been better even, than the tubercular
sanatorium of D.H., to remember

all of the south of France is to remember. Whites and blues
in incredible light, glanced off the olive leaves—it was
Matisse who said blue could act on the feelings like a
sharp blow on a gong, that the artist must sound, when
he must;

that olive trees are beautiful, but oppressive. He thought
Cezanne did olive trees okay, but missed the glare (which we
all found unbearable) wrote of the light as being "silvery"
and of style: it comes from the order and nobility of the
artist's mind, either acquired or intuitive—

order being what his housekeeper, Jacqueline most remembered
later—nothing about Matisse was haphazard, she says how
pillows, doorhandles must be neat, a certain way and O
if the tip of his cigarillo fell into the sheets and burned a
hole, O, O, *le maitre* insists we do not patch it, it's to be

an embroidered eye of the day, a daisy, never a hole.

CERTAIN PICASSOS BRING GREAT FEAR—
VISITATIONS OF AUNT RILLA

        Alden Park Manor, Germantown—
where even in midsummer, the radiators
did hotness at you; some fault, deep
in the walls or the wiring hissed.
"Imagine," said my mother, awed
by what she called Aunt Rilla's "moxie"—
"She tore down those walls, and threw
two apartments together; Fred's
into that wheelchair forever ..."
leery. "She says they need
room for ramps."

        Certain shades of orange
remind me of Aunt Rilla
and certain shades of blue, Picasso's—
her huge breasts, tumbled into hibiscus-
printed silk. Dream nights, I'm
hiding deep in pillows, or drowning
and I watch the lumber splinter
fractured, as Aunt Rilla claws the plaster—
fingers bright, and awful, with
diamond facets. Lights.

THE DOORMAT VARIATIONS

As a young man, Cummings moved to Greenwich Village to paint. ... At the easel or the typewriter, he liked to experiment with what he called 'presentative' art. He first exhibited his work in 1919 a the New York Society of Independent Artists; he entered two works, one called 'Sound,' one called 'Noise.' In 1926 he entered a doormat.
J.D. McClatchey, *Poets on Painters*

1. E.E. Hangs The Doormat

how hum humble i
preScent this oso   odor? no
        a
        f
        l
        a
        t
        n
        e
        s
        s
justthissideof
        plat
          i
      tude

2. Dr. William Carlos Williams Zips In From New Jersey And Dashes Off Tentative Notes

so much impends
upon

a limp door
mat

grazed by muddied
shoes

beside the silver
pigeons?

3. WALLACE STEVENS, ON COFFEEBREAK STEPS IN FOR A BRIEF LOOK-SEE

My Lord the tall Monsieur, who looms
into this chaos of museum rooms—
habitual quoter of himself—tut-tuts a shrewd
"'nuncle, this plainly won't do.'"
Goes on, "What we have here, if you please
are the usual 'lutenists

for fleas'; slat shank *femmes* galore, and now this
moribund from someone's floor, material
inscrutable, from a 'bleak
inscrutable shore.'" He sings
and in his song, lush fruits and vegetable stuffs
abound, with colored silks and hemp

piled high, in tuned rebuke
of dull, expected *tempi*. He longs for yellower
clumps, bananas lickering purple tongues;
dreams a sweat of watermelon pink
on ivory teeth; his lust
demands vermilion hibiscus, *en masse*.

But this. A mat precisely angular
confronts his eyes' templation.
There's also this: Monsieur considers verse.
Or, no. Perhaps a trenchant *carte postale*
penned to the sometime friend, the hanger
with a pungent question:

Bist du Champing at the bit?
Is this, one fears, a now ubiquitous
Declaration, the Death of Dada, dead as
Marcel's doornails, or what?
Use your imagination
and erase it.

Hang the moon upon a wall, light
reflective in, or refracted from, but not
a doormat. There's no discovery
nor joy nor pleasure in nonabstractness
of this sort. Quotes
himself again: "My friend, 'To impose /

is not to discover.' This is
no inconsiderable thing." Repeats:
"'It must give pleasure.'" Relieved, he plays
cerebral, with finer imagery; he juggles
seven globes of purest crystal
as he walks away.

4. MS. EDNA MILLAY, OF THE VILLAGE IS BEMUSED BY THE DOORMAT

Our hunchback garret room, Love, our tin roof
where rain and vines together tipped their dance
in tune with love's embrace—you, now aloof
no doubt forget. But daily, I advance
more deeply into murky memories
that shift from solid objects, random glimpsed—
this mat, a china pot, chintz curtains, breeze
that moves the curtains like a hand—such dense
constructions of familiars from a dream.
And this is just: our covert love consumed
itself, unnoticed. Half unreal, it seemed
a faded lilac, in the dormers' gloom.
It's proper dues—this haunted mat, and such
rude relics as your stubbled face, your touch.

5. MS. MARIANNE MOORE CRITIQUES THE HANGING

This doormat: I too dislike it. It is to fiddle with
    trivia.
      Seeing it, however, out of its normal habitat, one discovers
      a new perspective on rubber. The genuine
        artifact. Nubble that can clean a sole. Grippers
        that can hold the floor. These things
          have importance, not because
a well-known artist has hung this but because as article, it
          is
      useful. Not to be overly derivative, yet the intelligible
      artist knows "it is the particularization of the universal
        that is important"—
          the urinal of Richard Mutt
            the catcher's mitt
              the tail of
the cow that swats a fly. A field of verbiage, or dreck.
Nor is it valid to discriminate against
      "the sublimely pure concavity of
      your washbowls. The tubular
      dynamics of your cigarettes." One must make
          distinction
      however. When dragged into prominence by quasi-artists
      trash
          may still be trash. If on the other hand
you are interested in vitality of presentation, the literal
inspection of "all the glory that or which was Greece
          all the grandja
            that was dada" that's Art and
      this
          may be of interest.

6. ARCHY TYPES A NOTE TO MR MARQUIS AFTER CLOSING THE ARTISTS' SHOW

well boss we did like you said
and came to this hall
to check out the eats but
some tom cat hungrier than mehitabel
was there being arty farty
and you know after that time in paris
she wont put up with any of that
i who knew mike angelo in my other life
was not much impressed either
who do you think you are buddy she snarled
i will bite you and give you hydrophobia
the hors doeuvers here aint worth a nickle
he said and left but then
a janitor came in who had a big broom
look at this stuff he screamed
just look look look
we looked but it wasn't much
like the critic says we may not know
much about art but we knows what we likes
whos art to say anyhow asks mehitabel
toujours gai as always
but that janitor was getting red
swinging that broom around
dam fool commie pinko socalled
artists he yelled look look look a doormat
thats just nuts dam it all to you know where
he was still yelling as we crept away
they wouldn't get away with that
bang bang boom
if they had my wife

i admire his spirit
but his sweeping left a little
to be desired like the old cat says
everybody's a critic these days
humbug

archy

7. AFTER READING COMMENTS BY HER FRIEND CARL VON VECHTEN, AS MS. G. STEIN FIRES OFF A TRANSATLANTIC CABLE:

Doormats are not natural. STOP. I would adore a door but he should not hang a door. STOP. All the world adores a door. STOP. A doormat no. STOP. There are also door stops. STOP. A doormat lies very flat. STOP. That is what a doormat does. STOP. Some are thinking open or a beginning. STOP. This is not that. STOP. Ask any dog. STOP. Dogs are always thinking about doors. STOP. Some are open some are not. STOP. Indoors dogs are thinking outdoors. STOP. This dog is preparing in or out always. STOP. A mat looks like a mat even to a dog but on a wall it may not. STOP. And always outdoor dogs are thinking indoors. STOP. This is a opening or a beginning. STOP. A mat is something to be got around. STOP. A sculpture. STOP. I would myself prefer a painting of a mat to that.

8. E.E.'S FRIEND LITTLE JOE GOULD PENS A POEM FOR HIS ORAL HISTORY OF THE WORLD AND HAS THE LAST WORD

e.e.s mat
smelt some of rat
they thot & thot
of diddle squat
but what is sad:
it wasn't bot.

KEY WEST / STEVENS PAPER: FIRST NOTES

"Hemingway didn't like him."
    Ed Crusoe, Harbor Pilot, Poet

Her friend, the Harbor Pilot-Poet, Ed pretends
abysmal depths of ignorance in Stevens' lore;

encourages research. She's loath but flexible—
an easier sell than Elsie Stevens

who misliked travel. X and artifice combine
to frond a grove of palmtrees, sea-side

in her mind. Hibiscus, lemon-gold in green
she sees, and a vermilion moonrise. But what of this

ephemera are constructs for the erudite?
—My dear friend, Ed. she makes protest

—palacio of pizza and the fast food chain
have overdumped the Poet's walk: there's no gist to it.

She hesitates.—And yet, if one could prove a link
perhaps, a fruitful passageway to dazzle

the Professorial at breakfast; if one could demonstrate
an influence Floridian ... (pops up 'Venereal')

where Someone puts That Pineapple together ....
Ed speaks of clams, crabs' legs, and chicken thighs

some Cuban place the other side of town—
zarzuela with black mussels, and a yeasty bread

fresh-baked, they press as on a tailor's sleeve-board.
She sighs; she's touched by saffron dreams of rice

but adamant, insists on knowledge.
—Prove to me, she begs, that pineapple's Key West's

and no some cold-climed evanescence out
of A.&P., Connecticut.

Ed offers wine. Perverse, her mind deletes
"incarnadine," for local purple-gray of muscadine.

That sea's her artifact, her song; its image
dolphin-clappered, leaps to life

with azure cusps, white-crested; its host
leviathan, here barnacle-bedizened, beady-eyed

in skuzz of brine. (She notes how often flesh
incites the intellect to lust

for topic paragraphs *par excellance*
on "Aspects of ...." resists that tingle

of the antediluvian rush to imitate, to form.
Afraid, she's fainting on the fictive shores of Yes

murmurs, Melvillian—'Something further
may follow of this Masquerade.'

POST CARD JOTTING, SIDE ROAD, WITH JONAH AT THE QUI-SI-SANA HOTEL COFFEE SHOP

Green Cove Springs, Florida

   Bright morning, one of clarity. Clean air
fresh with smells of grits and bacon, coffee and
how we puzzled over the word "quiddity," deciding
it had something to do with a sense of essences—
One admires Ms. Bishop's "quiddity;" that came up
and "up," too, as a verb: the dog jogs by
his bannered tail upped with arrogance ....
a *quid pro quo* for you. Across the road
a barber buzzed a bent neckline, and in the yard
   there were mirror shards among the cobbles
where the boy had watered. Wisteria wrenched
arthritic knuckles on the sill, the sun-gold
stucco. We were moved to speak of Beauty, but
lightly, where "lightly," and "po-litely"
   and "quiddity" converged.

THE PERPETUAL MOTH

*He thinks the moon is a small hole at the top of the sky,
proving the sky quite useless for protection.*
          Elizabeth Bishop, "The Man-Moth"

            There's a relative error here
for starters: coming at it slantwise, eyes squinched for seeing
I think the Man Ray photograph's captioned "The Perpetual Moth."
But it's "Motif." Clearly, "Perpetual Motif, 1972,"—a collage
that collapses in my head with Bishop's misread man-moth: "his
shadow dragging like a photographer's cloth," that other errata,
the newspaper's misprint, man-made invitation to wander
parallel courses. This, they say, is Art made of metronome and
            "an omniscient eye." The caption explains
Man Ray's dilemma. Originally titled "The Object To Be Destroyed"
the eye which (as motif) winks here in three distinct positions of
the lens' mirror vision—on the left, tick, middle tock and right, a tick
again—is supposed to represent the eye of God, created in man's image
"a brilliant parody of terminism." It says. Ah, me. In 1932, however
he changed his title. The photo became "The Object of Destruction."
And one eye only, now impaled on the metronome's wagging stem.
            The plot thickens. (I'm easily confused.) It sits
(the metronome) a stolid pyramid heavily black on white much like
the green one on dollar bills in the Great Seal's motto, to represent—
it says here—A New Order of Things. I'm not sure I follow. "Motif,"
I understand, is something that will be repeated. In 1945, the title's
changed, to "Lost Object." "Indestructible Object," in 1958; "Last Object" in 1966, until at length in 1972, hooray:
            "Perpetual Motif." They were all done in various media
says the caption, which is less a caption than a history. In the medium
of words, I prefer to fondle Bishop's Man-Moth as motif. He struggles
through his subterranean life, at the end hands over his tears to the poet—
The mullioned moth eyes' weeping may become my symbol, ephemeral
and timeless (no dates or places) or the moth steadfastly moiling
in search of light.

86

QUESTIONING TRAVEL: A QUASI-SESTINA
FOR ELIZABETH BISHOP

Think of the long trip home.
Should we have stayed at home and thought of here?
 Elizabeth Bishop, "Questions of travel"

 In this matter of existence
there's priority of choice: rather there than here
or to have been or not, elsewhere; to carry one's umbrella
but leave the cane; forget the film, for knavish knowing
gift shops, kiosks, waiting under distant trees—
elms or maples here, not feather-duster palms. One

travels, seeking film or aspirin, or better, to hear one
noted poet speak. To cope with all the luggage—one's existence—
parse life like a sentence. Set out the nouns like trees.
Here it's Massachusetts, and October. Leaves here
glow gold and orange, punctuated now with knowing
that's sumac, scarlet ... Should I carry the umbrella?

I might drop it, as he reads. This morning's rain begat umbrellas
up and down reflecting streets. I must hurry. One
o'clock bleeds into three. Gaunt facades of houses, knowing
isolation (like Edward Hopper houses) betray a shale existence
only guessed at, past brick walls upheld by ivy—here
better served, poetically, by bare-branched trees.

But I've struck Greek. I'm dreaming olive trees
gnarled, arthritic, that lift their silver-dust umbrellas
leaf by leaf, begemmed with up-dot blue colon olives. Here
for a moment, I see olive trees—not one

but groves, and probably not Greek. Some past existence?
with Cezanne perhaps, beside our slate-blue sea? Knowing

I have been there, stood on vine-webbed marble, knowing
also, as I stop here, it's a dream. These are vivid, northeast trees
reflected in this street. And that it's slippery. So's existence
caught in discs that slither voices, facades, and yes, umbrellas
and the shushing sound of fallen leaves. At one
I'll hear the poet speak. Now, though, it's my voice I hear

in dreams. I whisper crystal lies, a poet's memories here—
some Greek, some sea nymph's knowing
how the sea is, and all those blue dot olives, where one
feels the grasping heat. You must come, see the brilliant trees
this autumn, say the Worcester poets. Bring your umbrella—
It's colorful, but chilly, our existence—

Of choices, hers was "awful but cheerful." Bright trees
nod here, over gravestones. And "untidy,"* the poet's knowing—
glimpsed, or overheard, accrual chip-mosaics of existency.

*The quotes in my last three lines are from the epigraph—chosen from her own work, by herself—on Elizabeth Bishop's stone.

MILE MARKER 31, U.S. 1, KEY WEST

1. Once upon a time there were:

    a. A beautiful, if somewhat plump Princess, and her father, the King.
    b. A swan who disguised himself in black velvet blue jeans and shirt, who posed as a friend of Tennessee Williams although he was employed as a tour guide in the home once inhabited by Ernest Hemingway.
    c. A plastic seashell which, placed on sale on a cardtable in the Hemingway home, in sound of Gulf and Ocean lapping and passing traffic, resonated with quasi-honest indignation.
    d. None of the above.

2. Given the above information, it is possible to deduce that:

    a. The beautiful Princess was deliciously pleased to find that her father, the King was, like herself, both intrigued and repelled by the swan in black velvet.
    b. Chronologically speaking, there is some stretch of time warp required for the swan to have both befriended "Tenn, Love," in New York in time to hold his hand in those sweaty moments before the opening of *The Glass Menagerie*, and to have appeared wide-eyed, in Paris, at the Hemingways' door. But his gold lamé sandals on the Spanish tiles here reveal him to be pudgy of toe; however no relative of the famous six-toed and therefore authentically Hemingway cats.

Wayne Hogan

c. Daiquiris being sold at Sloppy Joe's come out of a machine like blobs of Tasti-Freez, and would cause the swan's friend, Ernest, to blush and / or make obscene gestures.
   d. None of the above.

3. Given the plausibility of detail herein cited, and taking into consideration the possibility that chains, golden or otherwise, may be used to paradigmatically demonstrate the viability of a Great Chain of Being, it may be understood that:
   a. The lecherous-appearing, red-cheeked lady from the next table who volunteered to take pictures of the Princess and her father was hoping that the Princess was really the Princess and not (as she feared) the Queen.
   b. A ghost or aura of Tennessee Williams came to the home of Ernest Hemingway and announced that black velvet is tacky, stolen ashtrays from the Stork Club should not be hidden in inaccessible recesses of bookshelves, and swans should remember, Sweetie, all this role-playing is hard on the digestion and nerves.
   c. The Princess dreamed a dream on Tuesday, and woke up saying "the down side of things keeps turning up."
   d. None of the above.

IN ROBERT FROST'S KEY WEST GARDEN

*On the Occasion of Its Dedication as a National
Something-or-Other, March 1995*

Green is growing here, incredible, mother-in-law's
tongue is *sanseveria*? did I make that up? and
out of peat moss, that's a horsehead philodendron
beyond which a large tree's roots drop down ...
is that boabab, or banyan? why do I know so little
about so much? green veins throbbing in shadow
with splinters of skyblue, blue with white clouds
sailing, *cumulous*? *nimbus*? great ships crossing

There is a poem hovering in all this green fuss
did I read or dream it? something about green pods
green seeds held in green slips, is that di-cotyl?
somebody's calyx, symbol, sepals, probing
remind me not of the grained leguminous growth
but of grey pulp, bi-valved, bi-lobed, a night
notion, the brain as grey seed and the spine—
a white root, limber, groping—there are places
of the brain, where light has never been.

THE JAMES DEAN VARIATIONS

1. Houses

somehow, stay in the mind, remembered—
a piece of a porch, a lighted window
rectangular light in the darkness: Jonah says
this is where Jimmy lived. This is where
he had people who kept him—not his parents—
    we are both fuzzy about relationships
but I'm impressed: they seem to know him.
O yes. friend of Jimmy's. Rode that
motorcycle. O you're always welcome
do come in, they are urgent
out of the night.

2. How Things Last

What stays on, long after
the kids are all grown up and gone
is some reminder: this basketball hoop
    nailed to the tree
or later, in town
we'll see how the house leans, lonely
on a corner of two-bit shops and stores
where Jonah says farm buildings were—
    sheds and silos—their house
his father built, where Jonah was born.

The long tall windows in front were salvage
he says, like the rest of the house, trash
lumber, whatever was at hand. God, he says
    I hated those windows; no curtains

who could afford curtains? the light
one naked bulb, hanging down
      and that light was brighter than heaven
he tells me. Here I was, a fat little kid
thought the whole world was looking in

I was dying, of embarrassment, he says
but I had my moment: James Dean
let me ride behind on his bike
and we found the sky.

3. ONCE WHEN I WAS

Natalie Wood, I wanted to ask him O James Dean
how did you manage to pick up that
bottle of milk and roll it
      O, like Jonah, like anybody
across the brow like a savior
delivering relief—O James Dean, our own
icon at the drive-in, already lost forever
it was something about the eyes
just like Jonah, dark
shadows of eyes
              saw too much, seen
too much; it was way later
a stout sleazy Queen down south
remarked O how remarkable, those eyes

get you in trouble, Jonah would sigh; wish
(he often said it) I had any other kind of eyes.

Remarkable: note the resemblances to Jack Kerouac.

4. AT THE DRIVE-IN, WITH JAMES DEAN

[Rebel Without a Cause]

who knew?
that movie's a thief
        everyone in it's grasping
groping, starved for love—
maybe we should have guessed.
Even the windows, sweating
with us, with them

who knew?
        Jim Backus in his
(that marvelous touch) ruffled apron
or maybe Sal Mineo, his eyes huge
              black sponges

none of us ever again
so alone together, so young.

MR. DILLON, ETC.

1.

Seeing notice that our Local Poet
one Doctor A. Dillon is about
to teach the Public
Shakespeare, I am mostly reminded
how meeting him, once
he was frostily insulted I'd
(trying to be funny) called him
Mister Dillon.

He was—like Victoria—not amused.
    "I am a Doctor," says he
"When you are a Doctor," implying
somehow, I'd never make it
"You too will be proud."

2.

    It was the Other
Mister Dillon I'd meant, anyhow—
the James Arness one; but time goes on
and the mind plays silly tricks.
Considering DOCTOR Dillon now, I think
mostly not of him at all, but

dislocated, up pops imagery of myself
seventeen, newly married, living
in Fort Wayne, Indiana: one night, Jonah

my young husband, took me to the movies—
this was before we even owned a car—
no Drive-In for us—

It was in 3-D, *The Thing*
with James Arness as a weird vegetable
creature—he stuck his arm out—
a living carrot—and the door
(a steel-sharp Vegomatic)
clipped it off, INTO OUR LAPS!
      and screaming
I yelled out "O, hold me!"

3.

Later, walking home
we discovered how hedges
can be threateningly
vegetable—"O, hold me!"

I giggled and he jumped (Jonah
did) and when I grabbed him
clutching his arm—hardly
made it home—that hunger
3-D, there in the dark.

POLE BEANS AND FENCES

My Grampa Moon was a farmer, first
but farming's tough
& when the gov't got into it
& went to saying what he could plant
& what he couldn't, he said
(approximately, because
he was a Christian) you can
take this farm
& what he did then, was
paint barns
but barn paint's tough
especially on lungs already hurt
with emphysema, from all that
        hay dust
from farming, that
& the paint spray ganged up
& sort of got him
he went to painting farms
& barns, the paint-by-number
canvases laid out beside
    the day bed.
He was neat, color by color
& then when he got too sick of
staying inside the lines
he left.

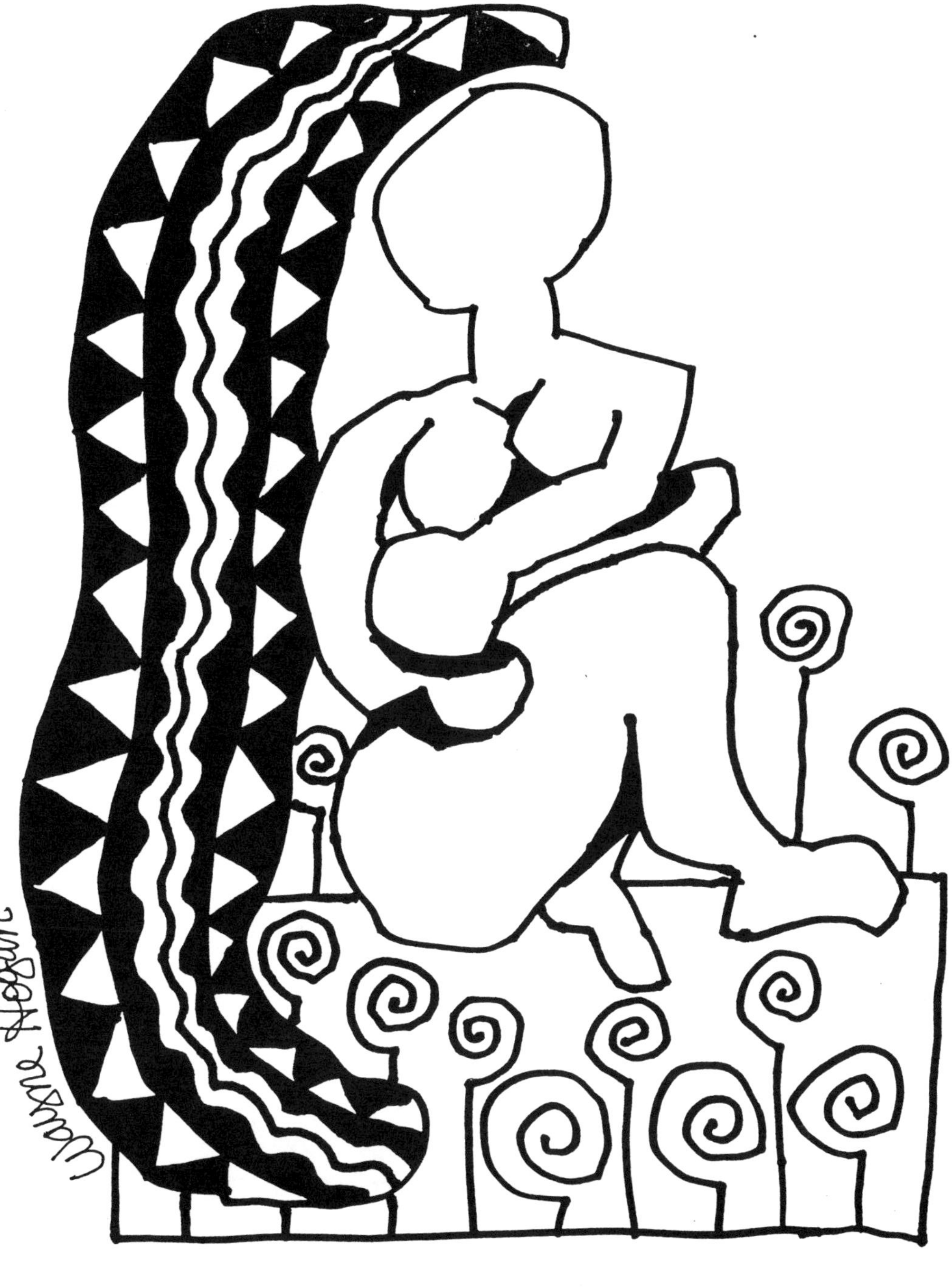
Joanne Hogan

NIGHT FEVERS, AND SOME FLOWERS

We're out on the screened porch, my dog
Lola and I, night dews dripping, making
      beaded maps in screen grids
the spiders can follow. There's
a poem in my head
and sweat, and the first line

involves the azaleas. Lola's sick too.
When the phone rang at dinner
she snatched a breastbone—
but that's no image for a poem. Azaleas
      will be better, to begin with
as the name goes *a* to *z*

and back to another *a*, a literal cycle.
The truth is always better
to begin with: here are azaleas
      in pink plastic pot
wagging dry flowers
to be plucked, cast out the screendoor

      providing mulch, another
natural cycle, hidden by night.
Here am I, in fever, and Lola throwing up
grins, clowning. It's her own fault
and she probably knows it. What's not
so evident are the seeds—the poem's

though the azalea sports tendrils
speckled with spores.

      They wag in the fine-veined
dried blossoms, ignored so far
by the bee-less porch.
      The poem's words

hum in my head, about death.
They start, out of the dark night's fever
beginning in my head, because someone
         some other night, in Kansas
was grieving for Ginsberg, sat down
and wrote lines in memoriam

and someone else phoned, from home
about Anne, my cousin. A farmer's wife.
      Aunt Bea said, sadly
"O Anne, she was always one to work.
They'll miss her, those fat sons
who survive her, and that husband of hers

      never says a word, never
says boo, you remember?" And I said
"O, I do," dreaming in this fever
pea fields, up north, long-lined fields
like my Grampa's, with the white-fluted
sweet pea flowers ...

much like azaleas ... this poem, growing
opens soft petals that flutter, lost
in fields time has taken
under blue skies remembered at night

  with no sound but spiders'
clicking at the screen

and Lola's panting. So much undone.
This poem's a fever to go on
"one last poem," says Ginsberg. "O let me
    clear up these last dishes," says Anne.
"Let me gather some lilacs for the table
some mock-orange from the bush

by the lily-of-the-valley in clumps,"
and behind her screen, in the fields
    the pea flowers, like white moths
flutter, and I don't know where it began.
With Ginsberg, or Anne, or Grampa
who died in winter.

"It's all words," I tell Lola. "And all too
too hokey for words. There's no poem
    here, after all." There's only night
with its separate fevers, and those spiders
webbing azaleas in morning shrouds
    in their plastic pot.

THE HAWK

For C., Pine Mountain, Georgia, May 9

I was waiting for you
   at a stonetopped table on a porch set into a mountain
   it could have been Chile, reading Neruda and Parra
   I dream of you in Spanish, *quiero que*—wishing
   you'd take me with you to Madrid or Paris
   and I drank so much coffee, waiting
   it could have been Rio de Janeiro
   river of my birthmonth
   the old full moon of the morning, decayed, led the way
   pale, through the strange blue denim sky
       and I was waiting for you
   watching a bird soar, high
   if this were Chile, or home, that'd be a fish hawk
   how his dark wings tip up, like fingers, hungry
   as he swings his circle, reconnoitering, the thin eye
   must glitter up there, circling, scanning for mice
   for squirrels, anything that skitters
   if I were home, where the surf sounds, thunder
   something reminded me of decks
   wooden porch slats, maybe, jutted over traintracks
       a bowsprit out of the mountain
   going someplace, over blurred green trees
   into a brilliant springtime sky
I am waiting for you
   knowing I must warn you
   know the table tips under impolite elbows

       it will dump the coffee in your lap, the cool coffee
       chilled by morning, the fresh morning I wait in
       wondering what kind of bird it is, soaring scavenger
       shark-thin, magic circles
       are there eagles here? some kind of hawk
       did I choose this place
               for the nature of its scenery?
       verdisima, very green, color of hope
       it is a dark bird
       it may even be some kind of carrion
               vulture
I will always wait for you here
     where the world moves like a ship out of the mountain
     where the trees blur, green and buttergold
          cool coffee
     and when you brush my face
        with your wing-soft kiss
     I will tell you to look out for this table
     we'll balance it between our elbows
     and maybe I'll wait three four days, to see the train
     tootle below the porch's bowsprit
     the bird, hawk or vulture, avaricious
I will always wait
     where I have always waited, at this table
     where I have never sat, before now
     where I will always stay

PAVLOVA'S DOGS

     Ho!
What a ballet!

improbable *jettes*!
     (Dobermans!
whippets, galore!)

    plies and
LEAPS! lithe bellies
upstretched, with just
the prickliest tulle

    TUTUS!

    and when the bell
chimes—*Alors*!

they are flying. Up
    into air, with more

Up Up Up!

    (greyhounds and
beagles!) grace
writhing up
lean—

she is smiling, Ah!
flips one hand Up
her toe spins—

Encore!

PRUFROCK, ON THE STAIRS
BECAME HYSTERICAL

considering the Cosmic
viewpoint: that sexual act-

    ivity's ludicrous
not to say trivial, so what

if I did or she said—
settling that infernal satin
pillow beneath her head

said Okay, Baby? Lordy.

The implications were
overwhelming, even
the thought of the diary entry
         "Okay, Baby"?

incredible. So. Home
he went, muttering
"April, it's April
(instead of Michael-
angelo) and it's
too cruel."

HAVING IN MIND ONLY COMMUNICATION ALEXANDER GRAHAM BELL INVENTS

the ultimate erotic
phallic symbol: the pole
and then there are
various connections like

lines. How those wires drag
to ring your bell, across
God knows what country
carrying this voice
this gossip, other words to say
really I am hungry for you
and would come through this wire
if at all possible, today
or whenever.

The receiver is very cold
in one's hand; the mouthpiece
to speak in is holed
for the voice; the earpiece
lets love leak

the soft word that curls
impotent, is goodbye.

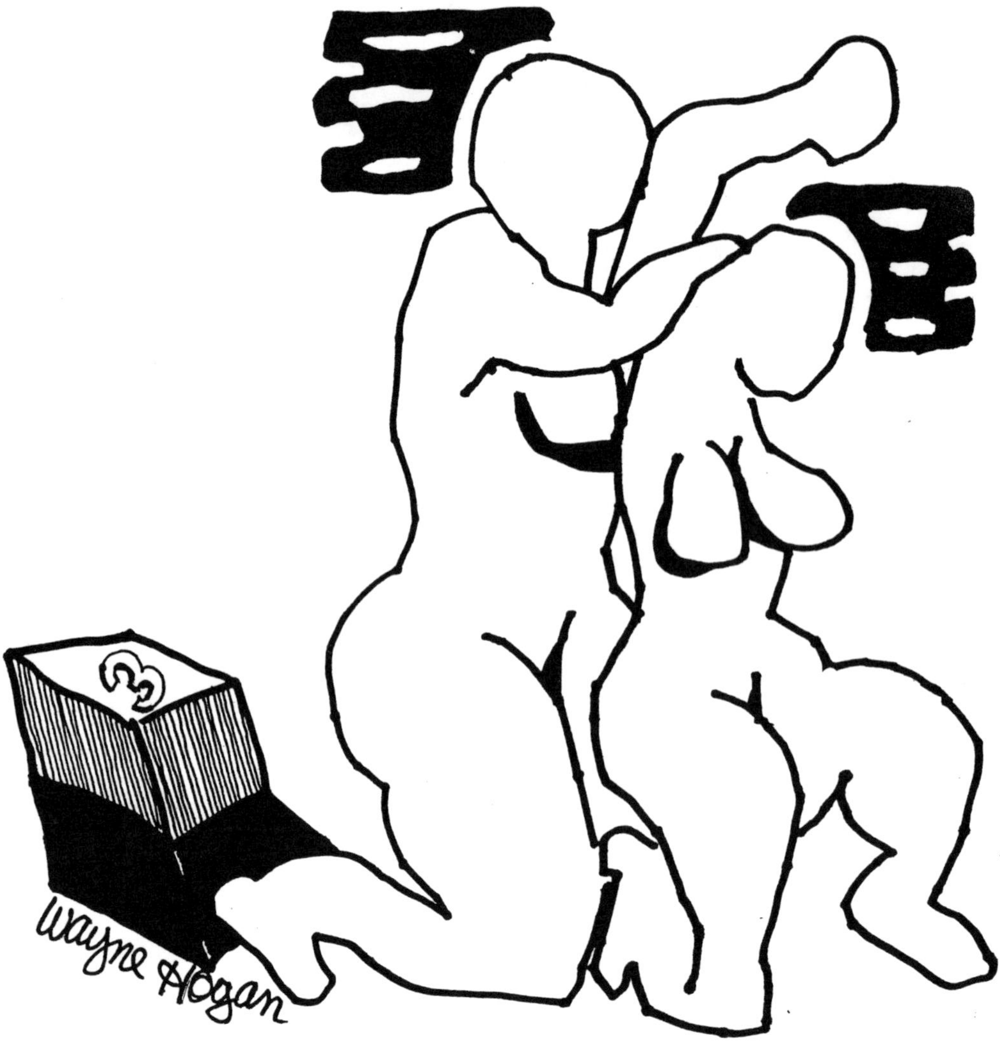
3
Wayne Hogan

ᴥ A NOTE ABOUT THIS BOOK ᴥ

When Ruth Moon Kempher established Kings Estate Press back in 1993, it was for the sole purpose of publishing her sixteenth collection of verse—*The Prattsburgh Correspondence*—for which she had asked Wayne Hogan to create the covers and illustrations. This book, her twentieth, and the Press's twenty-fifth, seems a special celebration. And very special recognition should go to Wayne Hogan, our friend and collaborator, who has done covers and pictures whenever asked, for not as much pay as he should receive. Also, all of our books have been typeset by Michael Hathaway of Chiron Review Press, and given their ultimate seals of approval by his mother, Jane. We are grateful on into the next millennium for their help and support. Finally, thanks to Sam, a good dog, who doesn't have poems in here, but who keeps us safe and loved. Wayne and his lovely wife Susan live in Cookeville, Tennessee and Michael and his family live out in Kansas, and all we do is put stuff together here in Florida. It is a gift of angels, no doubt about it, that sometimes it works.

– *ACKNOWLEDGEMENTS* –

Thanks to the editors of the following:

Abbey, for "Moment: Apocalyptic"
Amaranth, for "In Real Life, as In the Theatre"
Anemone, for "Reading about Boswell's Clap"
Artword Quarterly, for "Prufrock, on the Stairs"
Caprice, for "Kiosk / Gazebo"
Chiron Review, for "James Dean Variations, Part 4" and "Pole Beans and Fences"
Confluence, for "Looking up 'Ecpyrosis'"
Earth's Daughters, for "'More Apples!'"
Epos, for "Listening to Your Song, Studying," and "The Hawk"
Exit 13, for "Uncle Ike, Mover and Shaper"
Field, for "You're Quite Sure Then ..."
Florida Review, for "Wayside Flowers, Well"
Four Quarters, for "Cinderella Said to Her Ugly Stepsister"
Green's Magazine, for "Having in Mind Only Communication"
Gryphon, for "Gertrude's Poem,"
Hiram Poetry Review, for "Presuming on Emily's #341"
In-Print, for "Slides: Room 6C ...."
Journal of New Jersey Poets, for "The InventoryQueen," and "Unofficial Log ...."
Kalliope, for "White Herons, from Sunday, Monday," and "The Vine Fable," and "The Chased: A Revision," and "Beginning Her Clearly Mad Unfinished Journal," and "She Interviews D.H. L. ..."
Karamu, for "She Steals a Metaphor"
The Kindred Spirit, for "The Old Dog," and "Short Poem for Lili Belly"
Lamp in the Spine, for "Watching a Movie ..."
Loon, for "Once, When I Was Esther Williams"
Marjorie Kinnan Rawlings Journal of Florida Literature, for "Key West: Stevens Papaer ...," and "In Robert Frost's Key West Garden"
New Collage, for "Eve's Tart Answer," and "An Eternal Triangel: Hansel and Gretel ..."
New Laurel Review, for "Her Matisse Notes ..."

Old Red Kimona, for "Finding a First Poem for Jane," and "Looking for D.H. Lawrence in Taormina," and "Mile-Marker #1: U.S. 1 ..."
Red Owl, for "Pavlova's Dogs"
South & West, for "Thursday's Poem"
State Street Review, for "Apple Lyric"
The Village Idiot, for "From the Tub, She Teaches ..."
The Wallace Stevens Review, for "Quince, on Susanna's List," and "What Lola, A Dog Brought Up ..."
The Windless Orchard, for "The Three Little Pigs and Their Diets," and "Found Poem: My Mother the Typist," and "Looking for Kierkegaard"
Wormwood Review, for "Gambit" and "The James Dean Variations, Parts 1-3"
Xanadu, for "Leda, in the Classroom"
Yet Another Small Magazine, for "In Renoir's Dining Room"
Z Miscellaneous, for "On the Way"